LILIES FOR MY LOVELY

THE CLASSIC HANK JANSON

The first original Hank Janson book appeared in 1946, and the last in 1971. However, the classic era on which we are focusing in the Telos reissue series lasted from 1946 to 1953. The following is a checklist of those books, which were subdivided into five main series and a number of 'specials'.

PRE-SERIES BOOKS
When Dames Get Tough (1946)
Scarred Faces (1947)

SERIES ONE
1) This Woman Is Death (1948)
2) Lady, Mind That Corpse (1948)
3) Gun Moll For Hire (1948)
4) No Regrets For Clara (194)
5) Smart Girls Don't Talk (1949)
6) Lilies For My Lovely (1949)
7) Blonde On The Spot (1949)
8) Honey, Take My Gun (1949)
9) Sweetheart, Here's Your Grave (1949)
10) Gunsmoke In Her Eyes (1949)
11) Angel, Shoot To Kill (1949)
12) Slay-Ride For Cutie (1949)

SERIES TWO
13) Sister, Don't Hate Me (1949)
14) Some Look Better Dead (1950)
15) Sweetie, Hold Me Tight (1950)
16) Torment For Trixie (1950)
17) Don't Dare Me, Sugar (1950)
18) The Lady Has A Scar (1950)
19) The Jane With The Green Eyes (1950)
20) Lola Brought Her Wreath (1950)
21) Lady, Toll The Bell (1950)
22) The Bride Wore Weeds (1950)
23) Don't Mourn Me Toots (1951)
24) This Dame Dies Soon (1951)

SERIES THREE
25) Baby, Don't Dare Squeal (1951)
26) Death Wore A Petticoat (1951)
27) Hotsy, You'll Be Chilled (1951)

28) It's Always Eve That Weeps (1951)
29) Frails Can Be So Tough (1951)
30) Milady Took The Rap (1951)
31) Women Hate Till Death (1951)
32) Broads Don't Scare Easy (1951)
33) Skirts Bring Me Sorrow (1951)
34) Sadie Don't Cry Now (1952)
35) The Filly Wore A Rod (1952)
36) Kill Her If You Can (1952)

SERIES FOUR
37) Murder (1952)
38) Conflict (1952)
39) Tension (1952)
40) Whiplash (1952)
41) Accused (1952)
42) Killer (1952)
43) Suspense (1952)
44) Pursuit (1953)
45) Vengeance (1953)
46) Torment (1953)
47) Amok (1953)
48) Corruption (1953)

SERIES 5
49) Silken Menace (1953)
50) Nyloned Avenger (1953)

SPECIALS
Auctioned (1952)
Persian Pride (1952)
Desert Fury (1953)
One Man In His Time (1953)
Unseen Assassin (1953)
Deadly Mission (1953)

LILIES FOR MY LOVELY

HANK JANSON

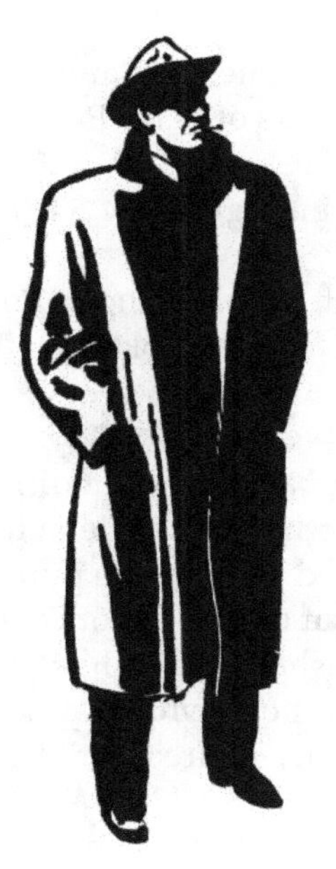

This edition first published in the United Kingdom in 2005 by
Telos Publishing Ltd, 17 Pendre Avenue, Prestatyn, LL19 9SH
www.telos.co.uk

Telos Publishing Ltd values feedback. Please e-mail us with
any comments you may have about this book to:
feedback@telos.co.uk

This edition © 2013 Telos Publishing Ltd
Introduction © 2005 Steve Holland
Novel by Stephen D Frances
Cover by Reginald Heade
With thanks to Steve Holland - www.hankjanson.co.uk
Silhouette device by Philip Mendoza

ISBN: 978-1-84583-870-6

The Hank Janson name, logo and silhouette device are
trademarks of Telos Publishing Ltd

First published in England by S D Frances, May 1949

British Library Cataloguing in Publication Data.
A catalogue record for this book is available from the British
Library.

PUBLISHER'S NOTE

The appeal of the Hank Janson books to a modern readership lies not only in the quality of the storytelling, which is as powerfully compelling today as it was when they were first published, but also in the fascinating insight they afford into the attitudes, customs and morals of the 1940s and 1950s. We have therefore endeavoured to make *Lilies For My Lovely,* and all our other Hank Janson reissues, as faithful to the original editions as possible. Unlike some other publishers, who when reissuing vintage fiction have been known edit it to remove aspects that might offend present-day sensibilities, we have left the original narrative absolutely intact.

The original editions of these classic Hank Janson titles made quite frequent use of phonetic 'Americanisms' such as 'kinda', 'gotta', 'wanna' and so on. Again, we have left these unchanged in the Telos Publishing Ltd reissues, to give readers as genuine as possible a taste of what it was like to read these books when they first came out, even though such devices have since become sorta out of fashion.

The only way in which we have amended the original text has been to correct obvious lapses in spelling, grammar and punctuation, and to remedy clear typesetting errors.

Lastly, we should mention that we have made every effort to trace and acquire relevant copyrights in the various elements that make up this book. However, if anyone has any further information that they could provide in this regard, we would be very grateful to receive it.

INTRODUCTION

By the time *Lilies For My Lovely* was published in May 1949, the Hank Janson novels were beginning to show signs of their subsequent huge success. The cover – by regular artist Reginald 'Heade' Webb – declared '200,000 sale' for the Janson novels, and that number was to leap by 50,000 a month over the coming months. That's not far shy of 1,700 copies a *day* on average – far from Janson at his peak, when he was selling 4,000 copies a day, but an incredible figure nonetheless for a novice author. Eighteen months earlier, Hank's creator, Stephen Daniel Frances, had been hoping against the odds to sell 40,000 copies a year if he was to earn a reasonable wage from his typewriter.

Lilies was the sixth book in the Janson series, written in early 1949 soon after Frances returned from a driving holiday in Spain. He had planned to make his way down the eastern coast but had dropped into the seaside village of Rosas for lunch and ended up staying for weeks. Sunny, friendly and laid back, life in Rosas was in sharp contrast to that in post-war London, and Frances was enchanted. A businessman from Barcelona was in the process of converting his neglected summer residence, bombed-out during the Spanish Civil War, into a block of three flats a stone's throw from the ocean. It was a chance that Frances could not let pass, and he offered to buy one.

Now, back in England, he needed to secure his earnings, and the next few months were going to be incredibly busy. The problem of increasing his productivity was partly solved by the use of a dictation machine on which to 'write' his novels. The wax discs were parcelled up and delivered to Hilder's Secretarial Agency in Soho Street, where an 18-year-old typist by the name of Jean was tasked with turning Frances's occasionally breathless vocalising into a typescript.[1] Frances would then edit the manuscript until he was happy with the results.

He still had to deal with typesetters, printers, paper suppliers and get his books to the distributors as well, but thanks to the Dictaphone he was able to write a novel in under a fortnight.

It's tempting to think of *Lilies* as Frances's first post-Spain novel. The previous book in the Janson series, *Smart Girls Don't Talk*, had ended with a bleakly pessimistic Hank walking through the streets of Alton, Michigan, having been falsely gaoled, embarked on a fruitless search for his missing girlfriend, Muriel, and identified the body of a young girl who chose suicide as a way out of the crushing poverty in which she was forced to live.

Lilies For My Lovely begins in sharp contrast, with Janson cheerfully strolling down the sun-drenched streets of Des Moines (pronounced 'De Moyne'), capital city of Iowa, on his way to meet a new girlfriend.

---

[1] In Chapter 6 of *Lilies*, a young, gum-chewing secretary to a private detective is briefly introduced, glancing at Hank over the top of a pulp magazine. The PI makes a passing reference to 'Joa— Miss Kaye,' perhaps a sly nod to Jean, his typist, and Bernard Kaye, shortly after to become one of author Frances's publishers.

Had Frances perhaps developed a new, sunnier mood? Unlikely. The story demanded that Hank start in high spirits so that he could be cruelly cut down within the space of seconds.

Which brings us to the central mystery of the story: how could a girl so young, so vibrant as Sally Taylor, die from heart failure?

Whilst there had been mysteries for Hank to solve in previous books, this was the first time a mystery had sustained the plot for so long, and the book is all the better for it, although nimble-minded readers will probably find themselves a couple of chapters ahead of Hank when it comes to unravelling the plot. It isn't so much that Hank lacks mental agility than lack of space for Frances to complicate the plot. With only 36,000 or so words to play with, the story needs to unfold quickly and race toward its resolution at breakneck speed, and it's very likely that the first person introduced who looks in the slightest bit shifty is going to be the bad guy of the piece.

Pace of both storytelling and writing also means that there is a certain feeling of familiarity about the plot and characters. As in all Janson novels, the slickest way to get into a house is through the French windows (even run-down apartments have French windows for Hank to enter); Hank often finds himself tied up in a cellar with one or two good-looking girls who are about to be tortured; and arrogant, stuck-up heiresses will definitely be brought down a peg or two and shamed into changing their ways.

Frances was learning quickly to produce the kinds of scenes that his readers liked, and developed this style of shorthand to move the plot forward quickly and allow space for other material. The Janson novels were not all

The 'seventh edition' reissue, with generic cover in red and yellow.

plot and no substance; but rather than waste time having Hank traipse around looking for a way into a building, Frances would use the space to paint thumbnail sketches of his characters and their relationships. The relationship between Janson and Sally, for instance, is marked by quick-fire repartee in the style of William Powell and Myrna Loy in the *Thin Man* movies, and Frances skilfully prevents it from getting stale too quickly by having Hank come out with a remark too far at the appropriate moment.

It is the strength of this relationship and Sally's charm and humour that engages the reader, so that news of her death grows in impact until Hank can drop the bombshell: he does not believe that she really has died.

Frances was becoming a master of creating instant characters-in-passing – a clerk is described as 'a solemn-faced, pasty-skinned dame, with a long jaw that made her look something like a horse' – and descriptions that helped ground the stories in their settings. The plot of *Lilies* takes Hank from Des Moines to Mason City, both real cities in the state of Iowa. Des Moines is some 300 miles from Chicago – which was to become Hank's base of operations once he was established as a crime reporter with the *Chicago Chronicle* – and 111 miles from Mason City (although the book gives a larger distance of 'all of a hundred and fifty miles'). Frances, drawing most of his knowledge from tourist guides, made an interesting stab at describing the architectural splendour of the Des Moines State House, portrayed as a: '… kind of minor White House. A beautiful building erected to satisfy the vanity of the businessmen of Des Moines, and paid for by the sweat of the thousands of Iowa farmers who really made the State rich and prosperous.'

The ultra-rare 'twelfth edition', with an alternative Heade cover. Only a handful of copies of this edition are believed still to survive.

The Statehouse (no gap) is indeed beautiful, with a high gold-gilded dome rising 275 feet above the 165-acre grounds in which it is set. Four smaller domes mark the corners of the towering building, which was built between 1871 and 1886 at a cost of over $2.8 million. Although it no longer dominates the skyline as it would have done in 1949, it remains a popular tourist attraction.

By dropping statistics and having Hank comment on them, Frances was able to offer the occasional polemic, with most of his ire aimed at the conspicuous wealth of businessmen in Des Moines in contrast to the grinding poverty of others (for instance, one in eight people in Idaho don't have a proper toilet). Doctors and morticians (or vultures, as Hank prefers to call one of them) are targets for withering cynicism, such as in this exchange between Hank and Dr Raylton:

> He said: 'Sometimes there may be irregularities when a patient's case is clear-cut.'
> 'You mean Dr Spiller slipped you a coupla hundred bucks!' I said.

Not all of the locations described by Frances were real. Clork Junction – where Hank's train is forced to stop when one of its passengers goes missing – does not exist, although there is a well-known Chicago railway intersection called Clark Junction, which might have inspired the name. Despite the inclusion of the occasional fictional town – such as Armidan City, mentioned late in the story – readers found Hank's descriptions of America convincing.

Another convincing passage in *Lilies* involves Hank's terror at being buried alive in a coffin. Frances was always good at describing the horrors of being trapped or enclosed, and it is the kind of fear that comes naturally to all. You don't have to suffer from claustrophobia to find the idea terrifying; a fact that has been exploited by filmmakers many times (*Diamonds Are Forever*, *The Vanishing*, *Kill Bill Vol. 2*, etc, etc). Frances had also written a similar scene not long before: if you are (un)fortunate enough to have read *Get Me Headquarters*, which he penned under the pseudonym Ace Capelli, you will know that he had the lead villain, Joe Keefe, escape from America to England in a packing crate – one of the few memorable scenes in an otherwise lousy book. It was written probably only a matter of weeks before *Lilies*, and there's little doubt that Frances felt the idea was a strong one and decided to incorporate it, with changes, in his next Janson yarn. Here the scene is all the more disturbing because the story is told by Hank himself.

Another disquieting moment comes with the tormenting of kidnap victim June Miller, who has been burned with a cigarette lighter on the bottom of her bare foot in order to make her sign a letter to her millionaire father; her kidnapper then threatens to cut off her ear … but eventually decides instead to cut off her hair.

> It was terrifying, frightening to see her. Her head seemed enormous, and the little irregular tufts of hair about a quarter of an inch in length that sprouted all over her head gave me a weird feeling that I was watching something dreadfully obscene … Somehow her face seemed to have changed and got out of proportion. Her eyebrows were just ugly exclamation marks drawing attention to the plainness of her features.

In a later book – *Honey, Take My Gun* – Hank remembers his feelings about this form of torture and uses it to obtain information from a female member of a Penitents sect who simply accepts (and actively encourages) being beaten as a form of atonement.

As usual, the treatment of women (and June Miller in particular) strikes the only dubious note in the whole book. Humiliation is one of Hank's tools of trade for taking people down a peg, but he also persists in the notion that when faced with a petulant and contrary woman …

> There's some dames that need slapping around.
> And the fella that does it is doing a them a favour.
> It might make all the difference in their life.

Although this wisdom is limited to women who are 'a pain in the neck', it contrasts starkly with Hank's oft-repeated opposition to violence towards women. By implication it seems that 'slapping around' is considered nothing more than a form of punishment, although where precisely the line is drawn between acceptable punishment and out-and-out violence is never explained. These were different times, when casual domestic abuse was unlikely to be frowned upon by Hank's primarily male readership.

Lilies For My Lovely is a superior example of the First Series Janson novels, its faults outweighed by an exciting plot, one or two grandstand set pieces and an engaging relationship for Hank.

It proved as popular as his other early novels: the first printing was probably 30,000 copies and a second edition followed within a few months. When New Fiction Press took over publishing the Janson novels, *Lilies* was at first reprinted minus the delightful (albeit generic) Heade cover – there are at least two versions labelled '6th edition' (mauve) and '7th edition' (red). In 1953, a '12th printing' was released with an alternate Heade cover showing a leggy blonde in stockings and high heels hitching up her flimsy night attire around her thigh. This alternate cover is thought to have been originally intended for the cover of *Milady Took the Rap*, which, when it was published in 1951, appeared with a plain red cover due to the intensive activities of the vice police at the time, who were gathering up dozens of Janson titles along with nudist magazines and other gangster yarns in an effort to crack down on obscene publications.

Janson was to survive this crackdown – as he says to someone in *Lilies*: 'I don't die easy.' Which could almost be the title for another of Hank's thrill-a-page adventures.

Steve Holland
Colchester, July 2005

1

The sun was hitting the sidewalk and bouncing back like an invisible heat-ray. I was wearing grey slacks and an open-neck twill shirt, and my jacket was on my arm. Yet I was so hot I felt burnt up, dried up and drained of energy.

But it was a happy day. The bright sun made everything colourful, and even black paint glistened and shone. As for the white stone buildings; well, they reflected a thousand little stars for every square foot of wall-face.

The streets were crowded. Businessmen wearing white ducks and panamas, carrying despatch cases in one hand and wiping the sweat from their brown faces with coloured bandanas, thronged the sidewalks. Brown-limbed girls, walking easily, looking ice-cool in short white skirts and linen blouses, added to the scenery more than somewhat. And everywhere there were tinted glasses for protecting the eyes from the sun's glare. Dames wore them, fellas wore them, bus conductors wore them, and even the newsboy on the corner wore them. I felt almost nude not being able to sport a pair of dark glasses myself.

This was the city of Des Moines, capital of Iowa, one of the greatest farming States in the whole of the United States.

But there weren't any corncobs growing on the concrete sidewalks, or fat Holstein cows grazing along the tarmac road. This was the City, the great City where smart little men with white ducks, panama hats, coloured bandanas and the inevitable sun-glasses, fiddled with papers, talked into telephones and made more dough in one day than a farmer could make in a month.

And what did they telephone about?

And what did those papers they fiddled with concern?

You've got it. They concerned farm produce. And that gives you the story of Iowa in a nutshell. It's a large State with only a small population. There are just over two million people in Iowa, and there's forty square miles of good rich farming country per head of every man, woman and child in the State. Yet only one man in five has a telephone and, worse than that, in the vast American continent proud of its civilised advancement, in the State of Iowa, one man in eight hasn't even got a proper toilet.

Iowa is the richest agricultural State in the Union, yet it's the same old story as you always hear. The men who do the work, scorch their backs in the fields beneath the burning sun, drive the harvesters and the combines, breed the finest pigs and cattle in the Union, those men, the workers, they get enough to live on, enough food, the rent, a rig-out of clothes from time to time, and maybe they have spare dough so they can come to town on the spree once in a while.

But who are the guys that have the real dough?

Who are the fellas that rent penthouses, drink champagne in nightclubs, wear expansive silk shirts, own racehorses and keep maybe two or three human fillies in apartments ?

You can bet your boots it isn't the farmers or farm workers!

No siree!

The guys who make the dough in Iowa are the smart guys. The fellas who don't know what a harvester looks like, who'd get corns on their hands if they took up a pencil to write their own letters.

When it comes to physical strength, well, they ain't got much to commend them except maybe that they've been eating the best food and as much of it as they want and sometimes more than is good for them.

But they have got the strength upstairs. They've got all their strength compressed into a neat, round ball and pressed into the oval of bone that is called a head.

And Des Moines is crammed with such fellas, and these fellas' dames, and their relatives and the hangers-on, the office workers, the poor typists, the gold-diggers, the parasites, the tradesmen, the thieves and the crooks

Yeah, Des Moines is just one more American city, loaded with grief and greed, pity and poverty, love and hate and fun and guns.

But as I walked along, I wasn't thinking of any of these things. There was a singing in my heart and a spring in my step. The sun was shining brightly and I liked it. I liked everything that day, because I was happy.

I stopped on a corner and bought a bunch of violets from a flower seller. The wizened old woman prepared them for me with a scrawny brown hand, shaking with age. I gave her a five spot and told her to keep the change, and when I saw the tears of gratefulness swelling at the back of her weak old eyes, my heart sang even louder, and I knew beyond all doubt that this really was one of the happiest days of my life.

I glanced at my watch and realised that it was time to make my call. I'd been walking aimlessly, waiting for the time to pass, wanting to make my call but not wanting to be a premature caller.

I turned and retraced my steps toward the residential district on the higher ground beyond the business quarter.

There were some fine houses here, big houses with maybe a hundred rooms or more and with private grounds that were almost parks.

But the years between the wars had taken care of many of these fine old houses, and great blocks of flats had reared themselves to the skies, just as imposing in their way and providing far greater facilities for businessmen than the old houses could ever have done.

I climbed steadily uphill and turned off down one of the broad, green avenues, passing beneath the shade of symmetrically-planted cedar trees. Birds were singing in the branches, and strong bright sun-rays penetrated the leaves so that light flickered on my face as I walked.

I breathed a sigh of happiness, turned up the drive to a small but neatly kept house and thumbed the door-bell.

While I waited, I looked around me at the carefully tended shrubs, the cactus plants and the imported rose-trees. It was a finicky garden, the handiwork of a fussy mind. And then I suddenly became conscious of eyes watching me. It was a sixth sense getting to work. The skin on my neck seemed to crawl.

I turned around quickly, half-expecting that the door had been opened without me hearing. But the door wasn't open. I stepped back quickly into the drive and looked up at the windows. Upstairs, the corner of a curtain moved. But it could have been wind that caused it.

Well, what the hell. Most people like to know who has rung the door-bell. Some folk answer the door, others try to check up before they answer the door.

I went back, thrust my thumb hard on the bell and held it there for slightly longer than was polite.

I listened intently and thought I could hear movements inside the house. It seemed an age before I heard the door bolt being pulled back, and then a lean-faced fella with silver-grey streaks just above his ears poked his sun-glasses around the door at me.

'What do you want?' he demanded, and although his voice was abrupt, I detected a trace of nervousness.

'I want to see Miss Taylor,' I told him.

He sucked in his breath so loudly you'd have thought it was the first he'd drawn for a week. And then he said nothing. He just stood there, sun-glasses peering at me, not saying a word.

It put me off my stroke. I'd called, I was happy, there was a song in my heart. And now this fella had answered the door, and judging by his actions he was upset at my visit – more than somewhat.

All kinda ideas began to revolve around in my mind, some of them self-insulting, others expressing hard and bitter feelings against a certain Miss Sally Taylor.

I stood there; he stood there. I could feel the tenseness of the atmosphere, and I was wishing I could see his eyes so I could tell better what was at the back of his mind.

At last I said weakly: 'Miss Taylor … er …?' I broke

off.

He said slowly, as though fighting for control over his voice: 'I'm Mr Taylor.'

'Pleased to meecher. You must be Sally's uncle.'

The start he gave was a very visible start. I saw the fingers he'd crooked around the door tremble like he had the palsy, and I swore beneath my breath, because it looked like Sally may have been telling me the tale; that this fella was her husband instead of her uncle.

I thought I'd get this over and done with. 'Just tell Sally I'm here, willya?'

He gulped. I heard him distinctly. The fingers kept trembling. He said, 'I'm sorry, you can't see her.'

'She's at home, isn't she ?'

'Yeah ... well, er ...'

'Excuse me, Mr Taylor,' I said firmly. 'I'm sorry if I'm causing you distress. But won't it be better if I see Sally?'

He said quaveringly: 'You see ... my niece ... Sally ... It all happened so suddenly.'

Some of his distress began to get home to me. I asked with too much boldness:

'For crissakes, Mr Taylor. What are you trying to say?'

'Sally,' he said. 'She's ... dead.'

'What!'

I stared at him in astonishment.

'Yeah,' he fluttered. 'I guess that's the way it is. Sally's dead.'

'What are you talking about?' I demanded. 'Sally Taylor can't be dead. Not the dame I'm talking about.'

He said in a sepulchre voice: 'It's very sudden. I ... I ... haven't got over the shock of it myself yet.'

I still felt he must be mistaken. The Sally Taylor I

was talking about just couldn't be dead. I said:

'I guess you don't understand me. I mean the Sally Taylor who's about twenty-two, height about five-four, dark haired, brown eyes, has a tiny mole on her cheekbone that looks like a beauty spot.'

He said shakily: 'I guess there ain't no mistake, mister.'

It began to punch home to me that this fella was telling me that Sally was dead.

I said, 'I was out with her yesterday,' as though that made it impossible for her to die.

'She died this morning,' he said, and his voice was soft and a million miles away.

A queer kinda lump came up at the back of my throat, and my tongue muscles seemed to be paralysed.

'Ya . . . ya. don't mean ... an accident,' I managed to say.

He, too, didn't seem to be able to control his voice. After a long pause he said: 'Not an accident, mister, heart attack.'

Suddenly the sky was overcast, the birds had stopped singing and the song in my heart had died. And people die too, suddenly, strangely, cut off in the full flush and vigour of life. I gulped.

'Heart attack?' I said, feeling the necessity of words but not understanding what I was saying, seeing only Sally's happy, laughing face, her wind-blown hair streaming behind her and her white teeth flashing in a wide smile.

'It was very sudden,' he said.

I stood there like I was turned to stone. Sally should have greeted me, laughing impishly, tugging at my sleeve, teasing me, dimpling so that the joy that was part of her would infect me so that I too was happy and joyous.

And now! Everything was shorn away. Those two words 'heart attack' could take away everything from me.

He was talking, muttering, saying something about finding her in bed, sending for the doctor. He must have been muttering without me hearing him. But I cleaved through all his mutterings.

'I wanna see her,' I said. I just wanted to have one more look at Sally. Somehow I had to make myself believe this had happened.

He was muttering something. But he was making no move to open the door.

'I wanna see her,' I repeated.

'You can't do that,' he said, and this time I heard him.

'I gotta see her. She must have told you about me. I met her yesterday. She must have told you.'

He looked vague. I put one hand on the door and pressed.

He shoved back hard. 'Stop that,' he said. 'I'm not having anyone come pushing around, tramping up and down the stairs. Let's have a little respect, young man.'

'Listen,' I pleaded. 'You don't knew the way it was between me and Sally. I can't go away just like this. I gotta see her, I tell ya.'

He summoned some determination from somewhere. 'That's impossible,' he said.

'Why?'

'It's all arranged. The casket is being taken to her home tomorrow. She'll be buried in the family grave.'

I gazed at him incredulously. 'The casket!'

He nodded, sun-glasses peering sightlessly at me.

Suddenly I didn't care about this uncle. I didn't

care about anything except seeing Sally, proving to myself what was so difficult to believe. I thrust hard against the door. Uncle swung his weight against me, and we struggled there in the doorway while Uncle began to call out in frightened tones.

'Doctor,' he called. 'Quick. Help me, please.'

Another face appeared in the doorway. A strong face. The face of a middle-aged man, intelligent, determined and dominant. He said in a commanding voice:

'What's the meaning of this?'

I stopped shoving. I looked into ice-cold, blue eyes beneath a high, wax-white brow. I said obstinately:

'I wanna see Sally.'

He turned around to Uncle. 'Haven't you told him?' he demanded.

Uncle seemed uncertain of himself. 'I tried to tell him, but he wouldn't go away. He insisted ...'

The doctor turned back to me, and his dead eyes rested on my face. He said coldly: 'Mr Taylor has been trying to tell you that it is too late to see Miss Taylor. Arrangements have been made for her body to be removed to her home town, and accordingly she has been already secured in the casket.'

I said weakly: 'But when can I see her?'

He shook his head solemnly. 'I'm sorry,' he said. 'It's too late now.'

A gnawing pain of emptiness came right up from my guts. I turned away. All around was grey and dismal. I felt my way down the steps like I was blind, and then through all my bitterness and unhappiness there came an urgent enquiry.

I turned around. 'Doctor,' I called loudly.

The door was just closing. Bui it swung open

again, and the doctor stood there, framed in the doorway.

I said: 'What did she die of?'

'Didn't Mr Taylor tell you? She died of heart failure.'

I said clearly: 'She didn't seem to me like the kinda dame that'd die quick like that '

He said quietly: 'Frequently they never do.'

'Thank you for your trouble, Doctor …?'

'Doctor Spiller,' he told me.

'Yeah, Doctor Spiller.' I looked at him. I hoped he might have something to say. Something that would help to ease the pain in my heart. But he just stood there, waiting for me to go.

I turned around and went on my way. And all the time, my mind was reliving the previous day. It had been an important day for me. A most important day.

The sun had been really shining then.

2

I met her in Des Moines, in one of those streets off the market. I bought some cigarettes, lighted my cigarette at the shop counter, walked out through the door and almost bumped into her. I pulled myself up and muttered an apology. She shot me a smile, a real pleasant smile, and passed on. I stood watching for a few moments, watching the swing of her white, pleated skirt above the brown legs and the rhythmic movements of her shoulders as she walked.

She walked well. There was snap and vitality about her whole body, a kinda animal litheness that was fascinating and alluring. Her white, high-heeled sandals set off the curves of her calves, and when the skirt swung, it revealed soft dimples at the back of her knees.

I wasn't going any place particular. I wasn't doing anything special. I just followed those legs. I followed them for quite a long time, and the more I watched them, the more fascinating and alluring they became.

I toyed with the idea of overtaking her and walking abreast with her, keeping level, slowing when she slowed, speeding up with her when she walked faster, until at last she felt compelled to say something.

Then I decided it might be better to see if she would drop in somewhere and have a coffee. If she did, I could sit at her table and maybe get in conversation with her that way.

Of course, I reasoned, she might be going to an appointment with another fella. It wasn't likely that a dame like her would be short of a beau or two. She might even be going home, in which case I could learn where she lived and maybe in some way rake up an introduction to her.

It was interesting just speculating on the various ways I could wangle a get-together with her.

But it was at this point that fate stepped in. That often happens in life. Just when you're figuring out how to accomplish something, the Gods throw the whole works into your lap. It happens the other way too. The Gods aren't always good.

But the Gods were good today!

We were walking on the sidewalk in front of some typical side-street shops. The shops had basements and the basements had pavement lights. That is, the basements were lighted by grills let into the pavement. The grills contained thick, obscured glass.

But not all the grilles were glazed. Some of them were just plain iron grilles, consisting of metal rods with about an inch between them to let the light through.

The girl walked across these grilles. She walked across four of them successfully. But the fifth one she walked across did the trick. She got her heel jammed in between two of the bars.

That was my chance. Even before she'd tried twisting her foot around to try and release it, I was beside her.

'Let me do it,' I said.

She smiled at me again. A nice, pleasant, comfortable smile, and I noticed the way her hair curled on the nape of her neck.

'Please don't bother.'

'No bother at all,' I said.

I bent down, got my hand around the heel and wriggled it. It seemed to be jammed down so hard I couldn't move it. 'Won't take a second,' I said, and I wriggled it some more. It still didn't come loose. I went down on one knee, got a firmer grip on the heel and wriggled and wriggled and wriggled. It still didn't come loose.

I looked up at her and smiled. She smiled back. She saw the way I looked up, slowly, my eyes travelling the length of her leg, and she seemed to like it.

'It's a bit tricky,' I said. 'Perhaps if you could slip your foot …'

'Yes, of course.' She bent down and unbuttoned the cross, strap on her sandal. Her hair brushed my face; I noticed her fingers were long and shapely.

'Rest your hand on my shoulder,' I said.

She put one hand on my shoulder and slipped her foot out of the sandal. She had a nice foot, dainty, beautifully formed. I looked at her foot, traced the soft lines up to the ankle, up to the calf, up to the….

She said sweetly: 'You were going to get my shoe for me.'

'Yeah. That's right.'

I bent over the shoe, got a good grip on it and wiggled it backwards and forwards. I kept wiggling it. It didn't have the slightest effect.

I looked up at her again. There was laughter in

her brown eyes.

'I'll do it next time,' I said.

'I hope so. I can't stand here like this all day, you know.'

She was resting one hand on my shoulder and she'd arched her foot a few inches off the ground. One or two people who passed by looked at us curiously.

'A good strong tug, that'll do the trick,' I said.

I got a good grip on the sandal. I tugged. I tugged hard. I tugged with all the strength I had. Something gave way, the sandal was free and I almost lost my balance.

'Done it,' I said.

The girl looked at the sandal. There was still laughter in the back of her eyes. 'Looks like you have done it,' she said.

I looked at the sandal and gulped. There was something missing. I looked down at the grill and there was the heel, still firmly wedged there.

'I didn't mean ...' I began.

'Oh, please don't worry. It's quite all right.'

It suddenly occurred to me that I wasn't managing this with quite the dash and efficiency with which a hero rescues the fair maiden in the story books. I decided to be masterful.

'You just leave this to me,' I said.

A taxi was cruising past. I gave him a shout. He turned in one and a half times his own length, missed another car by half an inch, caused three others to brake violently and drew into the kerb alongside me.

She said: 'Please ... What ... Don't ...'

I said firmly, 'Hold on to this,' and thrust the heelless sandal into her hand. The distance between where we were standing and the kerb was about a yard and a half. She could have hopped it on one leg with her eyes closed.

I said, 'You won't be able to make it on one foot,' and bent down and gathered her up in my arms. She was soft, cuddly and as light as a feather. My arm crooked around under the backs of her thighs, and her short skirt rucked up so I could feel her soft skin.

I winked at the taxi driver, and he bent out and opened the door of the cab. I slid the girl inside onto the seat and followed in after her. It had taken just about three seconds. Even if she'd thought of screaming, she couldn't have made it before we were in the cab. And she didn't look like she was gonna scream anyway.

'Where to?' asked the driver.

I looked at the girl, and her eyes were dancing. I asked: 'Where to? Where can we get shoes like that?'

She said: 'You won't get shoes like that in Des Moines. They came from New York.'

'Well, we'll get different shoes. Something much better than that.'

'No, please,' she said. 'You mustn't do anything …'

I turned around and said to the driver: 'Look, buddy, the dame needs shoeing. Can you take me to a local blacksmith who knows his trade?'

'Sure,' he said. 'I'll run you around to one of the best shops here.'

He started off with a jerk that threw me back on the upholstery. My knee brushed against hers, and there was a delicious thrill of contact.

She said, 'Really, I can manage with this,' and she held up what was left of the sandal.

'It's my birthday,' I told her. 'And when it's my birthday I go crazy. I just have to buy some dame a pair of shoes or I go screwy, like this.' I put my thumbs on either side of my temples, fluttered my fingers, stuck my tongue out and made a crazy kinda noise.

Her laughter rippled like bells heard over a meadow.

'But really ...' she protested.

'But really, I must,' I insisted.

'You are nice,' she said.

I sat up straight on the seat, looked her over very carefully and said: 'That's the kinda feeling I had about you. Can you imagine that?'

She blushed then, just faintly, and her eyes dropped, and I could tell she was tickled pink.

'When a nice guy meets a nice girl things can be very, very nice,' I said meaningfully.

The driver's window was open. I hadn't noticed that. He turned around and said loudly: 'I'll say so, bud. And how!'

I slammed the window shut. When I looked around, Sally's eyes were dancing.

'Say,' I said. 'Have you got a name? Something I can call you by? I don't wanna spend the rest of my life going around shouting, 'Hi, you'.'

'Call me Sally,' she said.

'I'll be fair. I'll trade with you. Call me Hank.'

'No, Hank,' she said.

'No, what?'

'No, Hank.'

'No, Hank what?'

'No hanky-panky,' she said.

I groaned. 'The first dame I meet that doesn't think that out, I'll build a statue for,' I told her.

'Poor Hank. Now he's upset,' she chided.

'You're getting too smart for me,' I told her. 'I'm

way outta your class when it comes to repartee.'

That nailed her. I almost overdid my sarcasm, because the laughter at the back of her eyes changed to angry flashes. I rushed in quickly and said: 'I don't think it's going to be difficult.'

'What isn't?'

'Thinking of the name Sally every day for the rest of my life.'

She arched her eyebrows: 'You seem to make your mind up awfully quickly about things.'

'Sure. That's why I always get things done.'

'I'm very slow to make my mind up,' she said with a twinkle in her eye. 'I always take a long, long, while.'

'Never mind,' I told her. 'I'll marry you just the same.'

The driver pulled up with a jerk that almost threw me forward off the seat. 'Here yah, buddy,' he yelled.

I got out, handed Sally down onto the sidewalk. She stood there with one foot on tiptoe, pretending she had a heel to the sandal, while I paid off the driver.

He'd pulled up outside a classy looking joint.

I said: 'Think you can make it?'

She grabbed me by the arm and held tight as I began to bend.

'No you don't, Samson. I'll make this trip on my own two legs.'

'Okay. But it's an awful long way to walk.'

'I'll make it,' she said. Then, with a sidelong glance: 'You could take my arm, though.'

I didn't need a second invitation, and I steered her through the swing doors into a fitting room.

The girl that served us wasn't so bad either. She was young, self-possessed and efficient. She spent most of her time bending down, trying various sizes of shoes on Sally's dainty feet, and I spent most of my time watching her do it. She was wearing a blouse with the top two buttons undone. She wasn't exactly a Jane Russell. But some folks think Jane Russell is a bit too much of a good thing anyway. Maybe this girl was just about right. I couldn't be sure. And I tried to make sure, and every time she bent down I was able to ponder on the question.

I was still undecided when Sally said: 'Maybe I'm in the way?'

I was just going to say, 'No, I can see fine,' when it struck me she didn't mean it quite that way.

'Er … er … 'I said, tearing my eyes away.

She was laughing at me, her eyes dancing, dimples in her cheeks.

I grinned back sheepishly, and when the assistant went off to get another pair of shoes, she said: 'You're the faithful type, I see.'

'Sure,' I boasted. "I'm the fella that can always be relied upon.'

'Better buy yourself a pair of eye-handcuffs, then.'

'I'm democratic where eyes are concerned,' I told her. 'I look at anything.'

'I had a different impression,' she told me. 'I thought you looked only at certain things.'

I gulped. 'Look, let's buy these shoes and get the hell outta here.'

'Anything to oblige old faithful,' she murmured.

When we got outside on the sidewalk, she stood there with her worn sandals wrapped up in a package and dangling from her fingers.

'Well,' she said. 'If you won't let me pay?'

'Wouldn't dream of it.'

'Well, thank you again and again.'

She hovered. I hovered.

'Well,' she said again.

I said: 'Don't let's be crazy. I wanted to talk to you. You getting your shoe caught that way was a golden opportunity for me. I feel something special about you. Let's go places and do things. I want to know you real well.'

'How well?' she asked archly.

'You're too smart,' I told her. 'How about giving a straight answer for a change.'

Her face straightened out, lost the smile and the dimples. 'I must be getting home,' she said.

My face fell, too, I guess. 'I'm sorry,' I said.

'Although,' she added thoughtfully, 'if you were to press me, I might agree to have tea with you someplace.'

'Will you?' I asked excitedly.

The little demon. There was laughter in her eyes again and the dimples were back in their right place. 'I'd love it, Hank,' she said sincerely.

We made a day of it. We had tea in the fairground in the bend of the Raccoon River where the racecourse is, and we fluttered on the gees. At any rate, I put the bets on and Sally did the fluttering. Two of her fancies came in, and three never reached the finishing post. Not a bad selection. She finished up a coupla hundred bucks to the good.

I betted scientifically, taking form and mathematical calculations into consideration. I was down two-fifty bucks on the day. I began to have a new respect for the pin with which she jabbed the list of runners.

After that I got my car and we drove outta town

to a roadhouse where we could get dinner, a dance and moonlight bathing.

It was almost a tropical night, and everybody was lightly dressed. When I danced with Sally, her body pressed up closely against me, I could feel the natural vitality of her beating into me. I began to tell her about myself, the things I'd done, the places I'd been to, and how I was working my way leisurely across the States with money to burn in my pocket

And all the time she tried to rib me, get my goat. It was like we were playing smart, talkie films, wisecracking, trying to give the customers a laugh. I enjoyed it. It kept me keyed up to a high mental point, because I had to watch out to see which way her agile mind was leading and try to checkmate her just when it seemed she was gonna turn my joke against me.

I said: 'You know, Sally, I think you're swell.'

She said: 'The first time a fella said that to me, I laughed so much I fell out of my cradle.'

I said: 'I bet you fell on your head!'

'No. I'd seen enough of men by that time to learn how to fall on my feet.'

'Ah. That explains it. The impact musta jolted your spin up into your brain.'

'An impossibility. I'm too high minded for that.'

'You're high minded!'

'Hadn't you noticed ?'

'You mean *you've* got high ideals!' Incredulously.

She said: 'A low idea never even enters my head.'

'Sister,' I drawled, 'what are you wasting my time for?'

That's the way we went on wisecracking. As I say, I liked it good. But there's one thing about a girl that talks a lot. Sometimes they don't know when to stop talking. I wondered if Sally was the kinda girl who didn't know when to stop talking. I hoped she wasn't, because she looked a real nice, cuddly dame, and right then I was wondering just how cuddly she'd turn out to be when the right moment arrived.

We danced a great deal and we danced well together. But jeepers, it was hot. There were three great fans revolving from the ceiling, but all they did was to whip up the warm air and move it along, just like a copper moving along a gang of strikers. The warm air wasn't cooled down any more than the strikers would be calmed down by the sight of a long baton.

She said: 'How's about a cooler outside, Hank?'

'Yeah. I could take some air.'

Outside there were long, cool gardens with hedges and winding paths fitted with seats. The moon was shining brightly and there was a smell of honeysuckle in the air.

We walked side by side, and I let my hand swing against hers. She didn't move it away, so I took her hand and squeezed. She squeezed back.

I stopped, turned around and looked down into her eyes. The moon reflected so that the whites of her eyes were silvery and the pupils were dark, mysterious pools. I didn't say anything. I just looked at her and she looked at me, and then somehow she was in my arms, warm and vibrant, her body pulsing against mine, and I could feel her skin through the thin silk fabric of her dress.

After long minutes she took a breath. I was feeling breathless myself, and my hands were shaking and burning.

'Jeepers,' I told her. 'You done something to me.'

'I'm not exactly an iceberg myself,' she said.

'D'you mind, Sally?'

'You can't see any tears rolling down my cheeks, can you?'

'What do we do next?'

She said. 'You go down on your knees, we take a fast car to the nearest judge, pursued by irate parents whom we beat to the post, you say 'I do' and I say 'I do,' and then we buy a farm and raise pigs and have three children and live happily ever after.'

'Hey, hold on,' I said. 'That's too fast for me.'

'I thought you were wanting to be fast a moment ago.''

I ran a sweaty finger around a damp shirt collar.

'I ain't got around yet to thinking quite so far ahead. But I think you might have something there. I'd like to think about it.'

She said: 'Let's have a swim. It'll cool you down. Maybe you'll be able to think more clearly then.'

'Yeah. That's an idea. I ain't never been married before. Maybe a fella should give a little consideration to it.'

'A swim will cool me down too. You know, Hank, maybe I did fall out of that cradle on my head after all. You're a nice, friendly, sociable kinda guy. But one afternoon is hardly sufficient to justify tying myself to a scrub-tub.'

'You won't be able to spend time at the scrub-tub. You'll be out earning my living for me.'

'You won't work me too hard, will you, Hank?' She said this pleadingly, with her eyes dancing with mischief.

'It'll be penal servitude for life. I'll never let you rest. I'll work you day and night!'

She said: 'I think we'd better get that swim.'

I went off to the men's lockers, borrowed a pair of drawers from the attendant and drifted along to the swimming pool.

Knowing what dames are like, I didn't expect Sally to be along for quite a time. I swallow-dived into the pool, swam deep down to the bottom, which was of glass and illuminated by coloured electric lights that gleamed rosily through the water, and then rocketed to the surface. Then I turned on my side and swam leisurely the full length of the pool. There weren't many people around, and I was enjoying myself, feeling the salty perspiration being washed from my body and the cool water flowing over me, restful and yet exhilarating.

It was some time before I caught sight of Sally. She was at the far end of the pool. Even at that distance, she looked pretty cute in her swim suit. The trouble was, some other guy had figured she looked cute also. He was trying to talk to her, and when she turned away from him he got around in front of her again.

I stuck my head in the water, started up the engine and steamed full pelt along the bath. I surfaced about a yard from the edge of the pool, got my hand on the side and hoisted myself out.

There was nobody else that end of the pool, and the fella had got hold of Sally's arm. He was saying: 'Aw, be nice kid. We kin have a good time together.'

'If you don't let go, I'll call the cops,' she threatened.

The fella sounded like he'd had a few drinks. But he was sure enough of himself. And he was a tough fella, too. I could see his muscles bulging all down his back.

'I won't hurt you. Gee, I just wanna have fun, and

you're a pretty dame.'

I said: 'Let the dame go, willya.'

He turned around like a flash. But he didn't let go Sally's arm. He looked me up and down, and a slow grin spread across his ugly face.

'Wanna get tough or something?' he asked.

'Nope. Just let go the dame's arm, that's all.'

'And if I don't?'

I could see where this was heading. This fella was tough, and he was gonna act tough. There was no point in wasting time talking. I stepped forward quickly and swung a left hard against his jaw. His head snapped back on his shoulders, but he half-rolled with the blow and took most of its punch away. I could tell right then he was in the fight game. He let go of Sally then and looked at me like I was a nice, tasty steak he was gonna try his teeth on.

'Beat it, Sally,' I said.

'I'm not going without you,' she said.

Ugly-puss stepped in then. He didn't seem to move quickly, but that was because he moved so easily. I ducked under a fist that scraped skin from my scalp, and ran full into another that seemed like it made a hole in my ribs over my heart. I went down hard on the grass verge.

Ugly-puss grinned, wiped the back of his hand across his mouth and said: 'We ain't started yet.'

I gathered my feet under me and sprang at him. He could probably give me twenty pounds, he was all bulging muscle and had probably spent most of his time in the ring. He'd beat me to a pulp if I was to fight his way. I didn't want to be beaten to a pulp one little bit. When I sprang, I intended my head to hit him like a battering ram. And it did. I smashed my head against his chest, and even his bulk and weight couldn't stand up to that. He went down with a loud grunt.

I got up first, waited for him. He'd got a quarter of the way to his feet when I uppercutted him. He may have known a lot about ring fighting. But he didn't seem to know much about brawling.

He spit blood and tried to get up again. I stepped in and tried to knock his head off his shoulders. He rolled his head with the punch, but I split his lips.

I should have know that when a fella doesn't learn the first time, he's pretty sure to learn the second time.

Ugly-puss started to get up for the third time. I stepped in ready with my uppercut and his feet lashed out. My legs disappeared from under me and I was flat on the ground. The next moment, a heavy fist smashed down on the back of my head. My nose hit the grass and began to bleed furiously and my eyes filled with tears. The fist smashed down again, and my face musta made a dent in the earth. I rolled, and the fist hit the side of my face. I squinted outta the corner of my eye and saw him, on his feet, both hands clenched together ready to smash down on me. Those two fists looked like two huge rocks. As they began their downward swing, they looked even bigger. I tried a surprise tactic. I rolled at him, knocked his legs from under him with my body, and then his full weight smashed down on top of me so that I groaned aloud.

'Quick,' yelled Sally.

I opened my eyes. She'd come up behind Ugly-puss, she'd grabbed him by the hair and was straining him over backwards, swinging on his hair with all her weight. I couldn't miss his chin. It was jutting out like the Rock of Gibraltar. It felt just like that, too, when I hit it. I thought I must have broken at least fourteen fingers against his jaw.

But Ugly-puss musta been tough. He sprawled over backwards, Sally dancing outta his way, shook his head, and then slowly climbed to his feet. I didn't try to uppercut him, because he'd learned how to counter that. I kept my distance, watched him sway unsteadily, and then launched myself at him again. I wasn't trying to knock him out any more. He was too tough a nut for that. But I thought I knew another way of dealing with him. When I hit him, we both staggered backwards a coupla paces. That was enough to bring him to the brink of the pool. I shoved hard, he staggered back, his foot slipped on the edge of the bath, he grabbed madly, caught me by the arm and dragged me with him. We hit the water with a terrific splash and went down and down.

I let go of him, but he grabbed me round the waist. I shoved my knee up hard into his belly, and he raised one hand, groped around my face, feeling for my eyes. I forced all the breath outta my lungs and sank like a stone. That fooled him. As soon as my feet touched bottom, I bent my knees, braced hard and kicked upwards. When I reached the surface of the water, I musta sprung out almost up to my waist. I sucked air into my lungs just as Ugly-puss broke water beside me. Even as he opened his mouth to breathe, I gave him a mouthful of knuckles. He went down again, leaving a dark red thread floating on the rose-tinted water. But he grabbed my ankle, and I went down again too. He pulled me down like he was pulling a rope, a hand around my ankle, the next around my knee, the next around my thigh.

He got that far and I got really mad. I kneed with

everything I had and punched with both hands. The water musta taken a lot of the steam outta the blows, but I was using a lotta strength. Ugly-puss had had some nasty blows from me. My two fists pounding against his already badly punished jaw was too much. He went limp.

I drifted to the surface. A few seconds later, he bobbed up beside me. But it was only his back that bobbed up. His head was still under. It was still under when he began to sink again. I grabbed his hair, held his face above the water and towed him to the side.

By this time, there were a lotta folk around. They helped haul him over the edge of the pool.

Sally took me by the arm anxiously. 'Are you all right, darling?'

I wiped a trickle of blood from outta my eyes, gently caressed my knuckles and said: 'Yeah, sure. That was nothing.'

'But it wasn't,' she protested. 'That was very brave. And you did it for me.'

Well, maybe I had. Maybe I hadn't. I kinda had the feeling that the way things were, I just had to do things the way I did. I had to ask Ugly-puss to leave Sally alone, and when he got tough about it well. I couldn't back down then. Not shaving every day like I do and having to see myself in the mirror.

They got Ugly-puss over on his tummy and kneaded him. He'd swallowed an awful lotta water, but he hadn't been in the water anything like long enough to drown.

I said: 'Let's get going, darling.'

'Yes. Let's get outta here.'

When I got through dressing, I made enquiries again. Ugly-puss was okay and had gone off to get dressed. I told Sally the news when she finally got her war-paint adjusted the way she liked it, and drove her home.

Well, I didn't drive straight home. There was a park on the way and … she didn't talk in the wrong places.

It was late when I pulled up at her house. She'd arranged that I was to call the next day.

That was why I was so happy when I walked along to meet her.

That's why I got a shock when her uncle told me the news, and why the sun stopped shining so suddenly.

And because I'd met her that way, and because I'd felt the vibrant, animal strength of her body, I just couldn't and didn't believe either her uncle or the doctor.

3

Even I could tell that the thing I needed more than anything else was a drink. I turned off into the first bar I saw and climbed up onto the high stool at the counter. 'Three double Scotch,' I ordered.

The bar tender looked at me, looked over my shoulder, and looked on either side of me with raised eyebrows. 'Did you say three, bud?' he asked. 'Yeah, I asked for three. And put 'em all in one glass, willya'

He looked at me with one eye, swivelled the other to the ceiling and shrugged his shoulders, all at the same time. His whole attitude seemed to say, *'I do get some nuts come in here.'*

But he brought the drink, and that was the main thing.

I took a good long pull, swilled the spirit around my tonsils, and swallowed it slowly so that it burnt all the way down. I knew pretty soon it would begin to warm my stomach and the fumes would be spreading up into my head, giving my mind just that little extra punch that it needed to figure out things that were baffling to me when I was quite sober.

Mentally I categorised all the things that I knew

about Sally. Apart from the general description of her character and physical attributes, I didn't know very much about her except that she came from Mason City with her uncle, the Mr Taylor I had already met, on business.

The house they were living in had been rented for a month, and they were due to return to Mason City in ten days' time. The only thing I knew about her was that her mother and father were dead and Uncle Taylor was her guardian.

All told, the information I had about Sally didn't even amount to a row of beans.

I threw back my head, gulped down the rest of the Scotch, and climbed down off the high stool. When I got outside, there was a shirt-sleeved cop patrolling the sidewalk. I went up to him:

''Is there a Registrar of births and deaths around here?' I asked.

'Sure,' he said. 'Which do you want, hatches or dispatches?'

'I want to see a copy of a death certificate,' I told him.

'That'll be in the State House Straight along this road five blocks, first left, then first right.'

The State House turned out to be a kind of minor White House. A beautiful building erected to satisfy the vanity of the businessmen of Des Moines, and paid for by the sweat of the thousands of Iowa farmers who really made the State rich and prosperous.

Uniformed attendants steered me through to the right office, and when I got there I was interviewed by a solemn-faced, pasty-skinned dame with a long jaw that made her look something like a horse.

'I want to get a copy of a death certificate,' I told

her.

With one single, smooth movement, she thrust a pen and ink under my nose and whisked a card from under her desk.

'Fill this form up,' she said crisply.

I spluttered ink all over the form, messed up my hands and the blotter, parted with a buck, and received a copy of the death certificate for Sally Taylor. I guess the doctor must have been in one hell of a hurry to register Sally's death. I'd been afraid that I should be too soon to get a copy.

I sat on a bench in the grounds outside the State Building and examined the certificate carefully. I was surprised to notice that Dr Spiller was resident in Mason City, Sally's hometown. That made me raise my eyebrows. Uncle Taylor was apparently a solicitor, and the other interesting bit of information was that a Dr Raylton had confirmed that Sally had died from heart failure.

I called a cab, and went down town to Dr Raylton's address. The further south we went, the leaner and drabber became the houses and the streets. When the cab drew into the kerb, it was outside a dirty, grey-looking house.

I paid off the driver, and then took a good look at the outside of Dr Raylton's surgery. Dirty, dust-covered curtains hung at the windows, and a verdigris-coloured brass plate that hadn't been cleaned for years was barely decipherable. I tried the door that presumably led to the surgery, and it was open. I stepped into a dark, smelly waiting-room, littered with scraps of paper, that had obviously not been swept for months or more. Nobody was in the waiting-room, and at the far end was a grimy door with the word 'Doctor' painted on it in thick black capitals.

The place stank. It made the hair rise on the back of my neck. I knew right away that the only customers this doctor ever got were suspect customers, maybe a fella with a bullet in his leg he didn't want to advertise; or a lady of easy virtue with sound reasons for concern about her health; or maybe a woman with a little matter of a miscarriage to discuss.

I curled my lip, strode over to the door marked 'Doctor' and walked in without knocking. The surgery was as grimy and as dirty as everything else, and a man who was standing with his back towards me hurriedly thrust a bottle into a cabinet before he turned around and gave me a bleary-eyed scrutiny.

'Dr Raylton?' I asked.

He promptly classified me as a potential customer. I saw the smile coming long before it reached his face. He had to do a lot of working to make it appear, but eventually he got his lips to twist into a greasy grin.

'Won't you sit down, sir?' he said fawningly.

I looked at the dust-covered chair with revulsion. 'No,' I said, 'I'll stand.'

I gave him the once-over carefully, weighing him up, assessing the calibre of the brain I had to deal with, and I was not impressed. His eyes were bloodshot, the sagging flesh of his cheeks was putty-coloured, his fingers were trembling like he was on the verge of an attack of DTs, and every tune he spoke he exhaled a cloud of bad breath tainted with the stink of stale beer and spirits.

I said grimly: 'I understand that you certified that a Miss Sally Taylor died of heart failure.'

I saw his eyes glint with suspicion, and the grin disappeared from his face like chalk wiped off a blackboard.

'Say, who are you?' he demanded. 'What do you want?'

'I'm a relative of the deceased,' I told him, 'and I want information.'

'Oh … er … well …' he stuttered, and he glanced over my shoulder apprehensively, as though to see if there was anyone with me.

I said grimly: 'You saw the deceased?'

He drew himself up indignantly, and tried to look like he was offended. 'Naturally!' he said. 'It's imperative that a second doctor should make an independent examination to establish the cause of death.'

'You examined Miss Taylor, and your findings agreed with those of Dr Spiller?' I persisted.

'Of course!' he said promptly, and he answered just a little too quickly.

I put on an act, allowed my shoulders to droop and nodded despairingly. 'Such a pity,' I said.

He immediately followed my lead, looked sorrowful and shook his head. 'Such a pity!' he agreed.

'So it was heart failure, after all,' I said. 'You know, doctor, I had the feeling that it might have been something to do with that hare lip of hers.'

'Hare lip?' he said, surprised.

I looked up quickly. 'Yes, of course,' I said. 'Surely you noticed … ?'

'Yes, yes,' he said quickly. 'But of course, a hare lip couldn't possibly have any medical repercussions …'

He wasn't able to say any more, because I was around the desk with both hands gripped tightly around his throat. I squeezed hard, and his bloodshot eyes began to protrude in their sockets. 'You slimy rat!' I gritted.

'You ain't never seen that dame!'

He was making horrible choking noises. I thrust him down hard in his chair, and smacked my hand hard across his mouth, and a fine trickle of blood crawled over his chin as he sucked air into his lungs.

I said grimly, 'Now you can start telling the truth, you phoney medico!'

He looked at me with scared eyes, but he didn't say anything. I gave him the back of my hand across his mouth again, just to give him the general idea. 'Start talking!' I said. 'You never examined Sally Taylor, did you?'

Again he tried to look indignant; it was pathetic in a way to see that washed-out remnant of a professional man trying to maintain a status he had lost many years before. ''We doctors confer,' he said, 'and decide about your patients.'

I said, 'You mean Dr Spiller came here with a death certificate that required your signature, and you gave it without even checking up?'

He said: 'Sometimes there may be irregularities when a patient's case is clear-cut.'

'You mean Dr. Spiller gave you a coupla hundred bucks!' I said.

He licked his lips nervously He didn't like being hurt, but badly besmirched as it was, he still wanted to keep his professional reputation. 'I examined the patient myself,' he insisted, 'and I am fully satisfied that she died from heart failure.'

I sank my fist up to the wrist in his belly and knocked his head back as his chin jerked forward. He gave a long 'Aaah!' of pain. I pulled out my pocket handkerchief and wiped my hands, as though they had been soiled with contact with him, and walked out of the surgery without looking back. There was no point in going any further. Raylton would insist on oath that he had seen the deceased and that she died from heart failure, and would support Dr Spiller all the way along the line.

Maybe I was crazy to decide to investigate the matter myself without putting it in the hands of the police, but I had the feeling that the cops wouldn't take any notice of my story when it was denied by two indignant doctors and Sally's uncle.

The next call I made was at a post office. I borrowed a classified directory, turned up the section headed 'Morticians' and ran my thumb down the list, marking off with a pencil all those operating in the Taylor district.

I changed a ten-dollar note for a hatful of nickels, barricaded myself in a telephone booth, and got down to business.

I struck oil with the sixth call I made.

'Is that Morrow's Mortician's Parlour?' I asked. Then: 'I want to make enquiries about the arrangements made for Miss Taylor.'

The girl seemed to know what I was talking about, kept me hanging on the line for a few moments, and then a dry, tomb-like voice echoed along the line.

'This is Mr Morrow speaking. What can I do for you?'

'It's about Sally Taylor,' I said, and waited expectantly.

'Yes' he said. 'What was it you wanted ?'

This was the man I'd been looking for. I said firmly, 'I'm the agent for the Ajax Insurance Company. I'd like to see you privately. Do you understand?'

He hesitated slightly and then said, 'Anything I can do to help.'

'Good enough,' I said. 'I'll be there in half-an-hour.'

It didn't take as long as that. Twenty minutes later, I was paying off the cab driver outside Morrow's palatial and ornate establishment.

The girl in the office must have been expecting me, because I was ushered straight through into Mr Morrow's private sanctum. He got up to shake my hand, and somehow he gave me the impression of a giant, black vulture. His black eyes, deep-set in his head, gleamed hungrily, and he had a huge, beaked nose that seemed to curve down over his mouth. He was tall and thin, dressed in black, and his long, thin fingers seemed permanently crooked, as though waiting the opportunity to rend at my vitals.

I sat down in the chair he offered me, pulled out my cigarette case, and when he declined, lit up myself.

Morrow placed the tips of his fingers together, looked at me calculatingly and said: 'Frequently we can be of assistance to insurance companies.'

'I'd like your co-operation on the Sally Taylor business,' I told him.

His hungry eyes gleamed redly, and then he looked at the ceiling. When he spoke, it was like he was reciting something he had learned by heart: 'Our business is a difficult business. Naturally discretion plays an important part. Our clientele respect our confidence, and naturally we take care that the good name of our client is maintained whenever possible.'

'Okay,' I interrupted him. 'How much?'

He stared at me with an injured look of innocence. If he had had feathers, they would have been ruffled.

'Aren't we a little mercenary?' he said, slightly disapprovingly.

'Cut out the smart talk,' I said. 'I want information, and you want dough. All I'm asking is, how much?'

He swallowed, looked at me calculatingly, and then swallowed again. He had a long, scraggy neck, and every time he swallowed, his Adam's apple went up and down like a miniature elevator. Then he eyed me calculatingly.

'To what extent can I be of assistance to you?' he asked.

I pulled out my bill-fold, extracted a century note and spread it out on the desk in front of him. His eyes gleamed like two live coals when he saw it. 'Just answer up smartly.' I told him.

'Discretion is very essential, and …' I cut through his burst of eloquence with my first question.

'When was the casket ordered?'

'This morning,' he said, 'early.'

'And when was it delivered?'

'This morning,' he said again.

'Did your own man attend to the …?' I couldn't finish the sentence, because I somehow couldn't talk about Sally being laid out in a casket. But Morrow understood what I wanted. 'No,' he said, 'my instructions were to deliver the casket only. I understood that Mr Taylor would be making the rest of the arrangements himself.'

'Tell me,' I said. 'Caskets have to be made to size, don't they ? How was it possible to let Mr Taylor have a casket almost on demand?'

Morrow breathed very deeply, looked at the century note, and said meaningfully: 'There are some matters affecting my business that I am reluctant to discuss with other people.'

I was getting hot tips now, and I didn't mind paying for them. I pulled out a second C note and placed it on top of the other.

'About the casket being ready,' I prompted him.

He looked at the black-edged blotter in front of him and said: 'It happened this way. About a month ago, a man called here and ordered a casket. He gave full instructions concerning the size and quality, and he paid cash on the nail. Within three days, we had made the casket and expected the man to give us instructions for its disposal. Regrettably we never heard from the man again.'

'So a customer ordered a casket, paid for it, but never claimed it!' I summarised.

He nodded.

'Quite a coincidence, wasn't it, that it happened to be just the size needed for Sally Taylor?'

'A lucky coincidence,' he agreed, 'although sooner or later we would have found a client who required it.'

I took up a new line of enquiry. 'Now what's this about taking the casket to Mason City? Are you arranging this for Mr Taylor?'

'I regret to say we did not secure the business,' he admitted dolefully. 'I might add that we have had every experience in the removal of the dear deceased from one town to another, and the subsequent burial with a suitable arrangement for pallbearers and mourners and …'

'Just give me what I want to know,' I interrupted. 'I'm not interested in buying myself a funeral yet awhile. Who's undertaking the removal of the casket to Mason City?'

'That I don't know,' he confessed 'Mr Taylor has

arranged for his own pallbearers to arrive tomorrow. My only commission is to supply a hearse for the transport of the casket to the train, and from then onwards my interest in my client ceases.'

I raised my eyebrows. 'The casket is being taken to Mason City by train!'

'The 12.30,' he told me. 'I understand the railway have been informed, and a special carriage has been allocated to the deceased so that due respect and solitude may be enjoyed by the relatives.'

'The relatives being… ?'

'Mr Taylor and Dr Spiller, I presume,' he said.

I pulled out another C note and laid it on top of the others. 'Mr Morrow,' I said, 'You look like and you talk like a vulture. I hate the sight of you and I hope I never set eyes on you again. But you have given me what I want, and I am prepared to pay for it. Good day!'

I don't suppose anybody had ever spoken to him so bluntly before. The shock of my words deflated him, and he was still gasping when I walked out of the office into the street. The sun was shining fiercely, it was hot and the air was dry and acrid. But somehow it felt sweet and pleasant after breathing the same air as that vulture

.

4

I had reserved my compartment on the train to Mason City, and I leaned out of the window and watched passengers scrambling into the coaches, and others who had already secured their seats standing and talking to their relatives.

I looked at my watch and it was ten minutes past twelve. Further along the train, two or three guards were standing expectantly beside a carriage that had been labelled 'Special'.

Then the stationmaster and one or two white stewards cleared a path through the crowds, and a kind of hush descended all over the platform as pallbearers walked slowly and solemnly across to the special coach.

It gave me a funny kind of feeling in the pit of my guts to see that casket being carried shoulder-high by solemn-faced men draped in black. And that casket was just about the right size for Sally, and I guess had I really believed Sally was inside it, I just couldn't have stood there and watched it the way I did.

The flowers on top of the casket were about two feet deep, and other pallbearers were carrying huge wreaths, almost as big as themselves. Whatever the true state of affairs, Uncle Taylor was certainly not spoiling the ship for a ha'p'orth of tar.

Uncle Taylor walked behind the entourage, and his white face seemed much whiter and his grey hair much more silvery than I remember them to be. He looked nervous and ill at ease, and was obviously exerting a large amount of self-control.

Doctor Spiller walked beside him and looked everything that he should have looked: tall, solemn, and showing due respect. Somehow the sight of them with bare heads and slow, solemn steps was the final touch. It looked like the genuine thing.

The casket was carefully handed into the special coach, the doors were closed, and the porters stood outside the carriage on guard in case any other passengers decided they'd like to ride with the body.

What I intended to do was really not very clear in my mind. Generally, I suppose, I had the idea of following the casket to Sally's home and somehow gaining an entrance to the house. One thing I knew beyond any doubt. I should never believe that Sally was dead until I saw her for myself stretched out in that casket. And if Sally wasn't dead, I was going to raise all hell finding out what had happened to her.

I was about to turn away from the window and settle down in my seat when, far off, I heard the wail of sirens. I turned back again to the window, listening intently. The sirens came rapidly closer and finally stopped outside the station, so far as I could judge.

It seemed like this was a red-letter day for Des Moines station, for a few seconds later, cops came on to the platform and cleared a path from the booking hall.

The fellow sharing the carriage with me heard the noise, and he joined me at the window. 'What's doin'?' I asked 'Is it a pinch?'

'No,' he said. 'It's the Milton fellow and his daughter.'

'Come again?' I said.

'You know,' he prompted. 'Milton, the pig king.'

'Is he somebody around here?'

'Not around here,' he corrected. 'He comes from Mason City.'

'Does he rate a police cordon, then?'

'Sure he docs. Any guy that's got a million dollars rates a police cordon. Civil servants don't really begin to get civil until you've got at least a hundred thousand bucks.'

Just at that moment, a small, pompous-looking little man, sweating from every pore and puffing like a grampus, hurried on to the platform. I gave a long, low whistle when I saw the girl walking beside him. Maybe Sally had got what it takes to get me het up, but I certainly wasn't going to rule out Milton's daughter as a potential Mrs Janson, especially since her father had a million bucks!

I stared just as long as I could, following her with my eye all the way to the coach steps. I stared specially hard then, because the steps were high and I wondered if she had dimples at the backs of her knees. I reckon every other guy there was wondering the same thing, because they were all trying to clear up any doubt on this point.

The fellow beside me said with a smile: 'And a million bucks goes with her, too!'

'Cut off a couple of 0s and I'll still take a chance on her,' I said.

'Me too!' he sighed.

There were no more funerals to look at, no more pretty dames with wealthy fathers, nothing more to see now except a few ordinary folks saying goodbye to their friends and relatives. I looked at my watch. There were three minutes to go before the train started. I settled back in my seat, pulled out my newspaper and began to read.

I waited until the train had been going for about an hour before I got up, stretched myself, nodded at my travelling companion, and said: 'Think I'll get a little exercise.'

He glanced up for only a moment, grunted, and then switched his eyes back immediately to what he was reading. He was reading the funnies, and it seemed like he couldn't take his eyes off them.

I went out into the corridor, looked out of the window for a time, lit a cigarette, and then sauntered down towards the special carriage. There was some kind of crazy idea at the back of my head that maybe I could bribe one of the pallbearers to let me peep into the casket. That was all I wanted, just one peep, and that would be enough.

Halfway along the second carriage, a broad, well-built man was leaning with his shoulders against one of the compartments. I just noticed he was there without really looking at him. It wasn't until I was right on top of him that he turned his face towards me and I recognised – Ugly-puss!

He saw me at the same moment, and I saw recognition in his eyes just a split second before he shot out his hand. Instinctively I drew in my belly and got ready for a smack on the jaw.

But I'd got Ugly-puss summed up the wrong

way. He was beaming all over his face now, and his out flung hand was reaching for mine, giving it a hearty shake.

'Say!' he drawled. 'You're the guy that I had a fight with last night!'

1 toyed with the idea of denying it, because Ugly-puss could be a very tough guy indeed, and I wasn't looking for that kind of trouble at that moment. But then I realised it was useless to deny it.

'Yeah! That's right!' I agreed weakly.

'Fella! I'm sure glad to meet you again!' he said enthusiastically. 'I looked all over for you last night, but you'd cleared off!'

Now if some fella had butted me in the belly with his head, split his knuckles against my teeth, toppled me into a pool and nearly drowned me, I figure I wouldn't be so happy to see that fella again unless maybe I wanted to return his attentions with interest.

That's the way I figured Ugly-puss should feel.

But I had him wrong. He wrung my hand like we were real old friends.

'Jeepers, pal, I've been wanting to thank you,' he said.

'Thank me?'

'Sure, pal.' He slapped me on the back. 'Don'cher remember? You saved my life.'

I blinked.

'You fished me outta that pool.' he said. 'I'd have drowned for sure.'

'Yeah, I guess so,' I said weakly. It didn't seem worthwhile reminding him that I was the fella that put him in the pool in the first place.

'I ain't gonna forget that, pal,' he said.

'That's okay,' I said.

He looked at me thoughtfully. 'I hope I didn't offend your dame, pal.'

'I guess maybe you'd had something to drink.'

'Sure,' he said eagerly. 'You know how it is. Once I get a coupla drinks under my belt, I ain't myself. I kinda get tough with anyone that's around.'

'I know,' I told him. 'There's lots of fellas like that.'

He said: 'Going far, pal?'

'Mason City.'

'I'm going there too.'

He didn't seem a bad kinda guy. He was useful with his fists, too. Maybe if I got into a jam I might need somebody like him to give me a hand. I said: 'How's about joining me in my carriage.'

'Sorry, pal, I'm on duty.'

'On duty?'

He thumbed over his shoulder at the compartment behind him.

'I'm Miller's bodyguard,' he explained.

I peeked over his shoulder. Miller and his daughter were sitting there reading. I couldn't see much of the daughter except her legs. The rest of her was hidden behind a large newspaper. But I coulda recognised her by those legs anywhere.

'I could fancy that dame,' I told him.

He contorted his ugly-puss into an even more ugly expression. 'That dame. She's poison, pal. Got a face and chassis that set the fellas alight. But she's got a mean streak so broad it'd take six cars side by side.'

'You don't say.'

'I do, pal. I oughtta know. I have to be around all the time she's around.'

'That can't be such a bad job.'

He leaned forward, took me by the coat lapel and said: 'Ever had anybody look at you like you was a bad smell? Ever had anyone talk through you like you weren't there? It gets you, pal. And that's what she does all the time. You gotta have a bankroll the size her pa's got before she'll give you a look that's human.'

'I seen them like that before,' I told him.

'Not like this dame,' he said. 'She stinks!'

Well, we stayed there talking awhile, and now I was talking with Ugly-puss instead of trying to put him on his back, I was finding him to be a genuine rough diamond. Tough and hardened, brought up in the bowery, coarse and ill-educated. But he was a good sort at heart, and was deeply grateful to me for saving his life. He pointed out: 'Most other fellas would have left me there to drown after I'd picked a fight that way. I gotta hand it to you. You got me outta that mess, fella, and any time I can do something for you, just you call on me.'

I wandered on down the corridor, swaying from side to side with the movement of the train, which was now moving at top speed.

About two carriages along, I came into the section of the train that had been reserved for the funeral cortege. There was a pallbearer standing at one end of the corridor and another standing further along. There was no reason why they shouldn't be standing there in the corridor getting some air, but their attitude did seem to suggest more that they were on guard than anything else.

I pushed past the first man. He glanced at me with dead, grey eyes set in a wax-white face. There were beads of perspiration lining his brow where the tall black hat sat squarely on his head.

I felt his eyes piercing into the back of my neck, and the other fella whom I was approaching watched me with the same dead-pan expression. I slowed my pace, stopped, leaned against the window and fumbled for my cigarette pack. I took some time selecting a fag and putting it in my mouth, and when I struck the match, I looked at the first fella again. He'd moved up towards me and was watching me intently.

I blew a spiral of smoke toward the roof of the carriage, and allowed the lurching of the train to swing me against the door of the compartment where I guessed the coffin would be. The pallbearer made an instinctive movement towards me, which he immediately checked.

Well, if I was gonna try anything, now was the time. I jerked open the window of the train, threw my cigarette out on the line, jerked up the window again and, before they'd realised it, spun around and jerked at the door of the compartment. It stuck a bit on the rollers, and before I'd got it properly open, both of those bearers had reached me.

One of them said firmly but politely, 'I'm sorry, sir, but that is a specially reserved carriage.'

I wasn't taking much notice of him. I was looking at the casket, placed neatly on the trestles and smothered with flowers.

There were another coupla pallbearers in the compartment. They sprang up as I opened the door and got between me and the casket.

I said: 'That's Sally Taylor in there, isn't it?'

One of them looked at the other and said: 'Sure thing, fella. But this is supposed to be private. Outside if you please.'

'I'd give a hundred bucks for a look at that dame,' I said.

The bearer who'd spoken looked meaningfully at the others. Gently but firmly I was crowded out into the corridor. 'You're the fella Sally met yesterday, aincher?' said one of them.

'Yeah. That's why I wanna see her.'

'You can't see her, pal. You can spill all the tears you want and flutter all the dough you've got, but you can't see her.'

I said: 'She didn't die of the plague, did she?'

'Be sensible, fella,' he said. 'Ain't you noticed how hot it is? This broad's gotta go to Mason City to be planted. That's a long way in this hot weather. We had to take care of that before we started. That's why she's screwed down.'

'Okay,' I said. 'You've convinced me.'

I turned away, made as though to put my hands in my pockets, sensed them relaxing, and then spun around and charged through them.

I got through the compartment door with my pocket torn off and got as far as sweeping the wreaths off the top of the casket before one of them got his arm crooked around my neck. I knew the answer to that. I back-heeled him, and he sank down moaning. But there were three others to deal with. And they were tough. I got a slug on the back of the neck that sent me sprawling across the casket, and another smash in the back that made me feel like one of my kidneys had been mashed. I elbowed one of them in the eye before they really got a grip on me, and then there was a mad, frenzied scramble for some minutes.

I ended up in the corridor, lying on the floor

with one of them sitting on my head, another across my legs and the third screwing my arm way up behind my back.

I groaned. I groaned loudly.

'Break his arm,' said the fella sitting on my head. 'We don't want more trouble with him.'

It felt just like that was what was going to happen. I guess they would have broken my arm, too. I was evaporating into a mist of unbearable agony when a voice I knew said:

'What on earth's happening?'

The fella sitting on my head got up. I saw Dr Spiller through the pain-sweat dripping over my forehead. The fella screwing my arm off hadn't let up, but he wasn't putting on the pressure any more.

'This fella got tough. Tried to open the casket.'

Dr Spiller looked at me. 'Let him go,' he said.

They let go of me. I didn't get up. I lay there. I didn't feel I could stand right then.

Spiller said: 'So it's you again?'

'Yeah. It's me.' I was panting.

'Maybe it'll save us a lotta trouble if we report you to the correct authorities and charge you.'

I got to my feet groggily, flexed my arm, and was surprised that the muscles and sinews hadn't been twisted into spam.

'You can go to hell,' I said and, turning away, I stumbled back along the corridor toward my carriage. The bearers made way for me, and I got a little satisfaction at seeing one of them with an eye that looked like it was gonna be a deep purple within a few hours.

On the way back, I passed Ugly-puss. He gazed at the red mark on my cheek, my ruffled hair and my torn jacket with amazement.

'Say, pal,' he said. 'Someone get tough with you?'

'Four of 'em,' I said.

An eager light shone in his eyes. He took his fists from his pocket and closed them into hams of iron. 'Let's go back,' he said with the gleam of battle in his eye. 'Between us, we'll do them.' Then disappointment spread across his face. 'I just remembered,' he said. 'I gotta stay here and watch Miller.'

I gave him a playful punch. 'That's okay. I can settle with them punks later. Plenty of time.'

He said eagerly: 'You'll let me in on it?'

'Sure,' I promised. 'You can help.'

He leaned back against the compartment door with a satisfied look. 'Don't forget,' he said.

5

It's a long run from Des Moines to Mason City; all of a hundred and fifty miles. That gave me plenty of time to sit back in my seat and figure out what moves I'd make when I eventually got to Mason City.

The thing for me to do, I decided, was to follow Uncle Taylor to his home and seize my opportunity of entering the house and getting that casket open. If, as I suspected, Sally had not really died, I still had to find out what had happened to her.

The fella sitting opposite me still had his beak buried in the funnies. Every little while he gave a guffaw. I leaned back, rested my head and closed my eyes. The steady tackity-tack of the train wheels on the track was soothing, lulling me to sleep.

It musta been an hour later when I opened my eyes. Ugly-puss was staring into the compartment with a worried expression intensifying his ugliness. When he saw me, he jerked his head, inviting me to join him.

I got up, went outside into the corridor.

Ugly-puss said: 'Say, pal. Have you seen June Miller?'

'Is that her name?'

'Yeah, sure it is. Have you seen her around, pal?'

I could tell that Ugly-puss was mighty worried. 'Have you lost her?' I asked.

'She's disappeared,'' he said.

'Nonsense. She must be around some place.'

'I looked all over,' he said. 'Old man Miller is going crazy.'

I said: 'You musta missed her some place. Maybe she got off down the line and missed the train?'

He said seriously: 'Listen pal. She couldn't have got off, 'cos the train ain't stopped yet.'

'Well, she must still be on the train somewhere.'

'I been through this train with a fine toothcomb,' he said. His eyes were worried.

Just then, old Miller came bustling up. His face was red with exasperation. He was leading three car attendants. He yelled out to Ugly-puss: 'Now, you incompetent fool, we're going to search this train thoroughly.' Then he glared at me. 'Who's this fella,' he demanded.

'He's a pal of mine,' said Ugly-puss bleakly.

Miller snorted and pushed his way down toward the rear of the train. Ugly-puss shrugged his shoulders despairingly. 'Wanna help me, pal ?' he invited.

'Sure.'

There were three car attendants, Miller, Ugly-puss and me. We started at the rear end of the train and worked forward. We went into every compartment, toilet and cubby-hole as we worked our way through toward the front of the train. We had a spot of trouble when we got to the compartment set aside for the funeral cortege, because Uncle Taylor and Doctor Spiller point blank refused to allow me anywhere near the compartment. They complained I'd already committed sacrilegious behaviour. But they let Miller and the attendants search the compartment, and then we continued right through to the front of the train.

When we reached there without having seen the slightest evidence of June Miller's existence, Miller's face had changed from red to white. He wasn't annoyed any longer. He was scared.

One of the guards said: 'You can see for yourself, Mr Miller, that she isn't on the train.'

'I can see that, you fool. What I want to know is, where has she got to?'

The guard shrugged his shoulders. 'If she ain't on the train, she must be off the train. And since the train ain't stopped, she must have got off while it was moving.'

I said: 'Anyone getting off this train while it's moving this way is liable to get a face full of sleeper splinters.'

Miller rounded on Ugly-puss. 'Now, you blundering jackass,' he said, 'what happened? Tell it again, just the way it happened.'

Ugly-puss swallowed, cowed by this pompous little man. He said weakly: 'Just like I told you, boss. You was asleep. Miss June got up, came out into the corridor and walked up towards the engine.

'Did she say where she was going?'

Ugly-puss blushed. 'I didn't like to ask,' he confessed. 'Folks always take a stroll down the corridor on a long train journey.'

'Why didn't you follow her and make sure she was all right?'

Ugly-puss was sweating slightly. 'I can't be two places at one time, boss. I was hired to be your bodyguard If I'd followed the dame, maybe you'd have disappeared.'

Miller snorted again. Then he snapped at one of the guards: 'Stop the train,' he said.

'What?'

'You heard me. Stop the train'

'Just a minute, Mr Miller,' said the guard. 'That ain't gonna do no good. In ten minutes we'll be running into Clork Junction We can stop there. There'll be a telephone, and maybe we'll get some news We can even get gangers out searching the line.'

Miller suddenly put his hand to his forehead. His face became terribly white and drawn. He swayed almost imperceptibly. Ugly-puss reached out and steadied him. I said: 'Get him in a compartment.'

We steered Miller into a compartment, and one of the guards found a glass of brandy. Miller, for all his millions, looked like a very unhappy man. He was going through hell. It was pretty clear he thought a great deal of that daughter of his.

Ten minutes later we ran into Clork Junction and the tram slowed to a halt.

Miller must have been quite a guy. It's surprising what difference it makes when you've got a stack of greenbacks piled up in the bank with your name on them. It seemed like in five minutes, Clork Junction had turned itself upside down on account of the Miller Millions

They got the whole station staff, half the local cop force and some plain clothes dicks on the job. They kept the train waiting for twenty minutes or so while every nook and cranny of it was searched It seemed like all hell was let loose on account of June Miller. Local newsboys were wandering around with their ears flapping, and already the word 'suicide' was slipping from mouth to mouth.

Ugly-puss said: 'The boss is gonna stay on here till we can get the line searched.'

'Don't worry, pal.' I said. 'She'll turn up. They always do that.'

'Yeah,' he said mournfully. 'But if she turns up in the morgue, my boss ain't gonna like it. He'll get around to figuring that it's my fault.'

'There's plenty of other jobs.'

''Cept, the only thing I know how to do is slugging guys. I ain't no good in the ring no more, on account I got a rupture. The only kinda job I'm gonna get is as a bodyguard – and I reckon Miller ain't gonna give me a reference that's gonna shine. And I ain't gonna get another job without a reference.'

'Maybe she'll turn up all right,' I said.

'I hope so.'

'Let me know what happens. Send me a line. Hank Janson, care of the Post Office, Mason City.'

'I'll write you, fella.'

'D'you know where you're stopping here?' I asked. At the back of my mind was the feeling that if he was given the push by Miller, he might earn himself a few bucks by helping me, if I met up with trouble.

'This is a dump. There's only one hotel, Morgan's Hotel. I guess I'll be staying there if we don't go back to Des Moines.'

'Who do I ask for?'

'I'm Dan Rutland,' he said.

Dan Rutland? Dan Rutland? I turned the name over in my mind. And then I got it. I said incredulously: 'You're *the* Dan Rutland, the fella that fought a fourteen rounder with Perry and was floored by a disputed foul?'

'That's me,' he said just a little proudly.

'I've always wanted to know.' I said. 'Did Perry foul you?'

'Well … I guess I dunno. We was mixing pretty fast, and it seemed like he swung hard at the same time as I kinda sprang high. Coulda happened to anybody. I guess the judges were right to give him the decision.'

'You ain't been fighting at all since then?'

He said: 'It's like I said. I got a rupture, see.'

'Is that what happened with the foul?'

'Perry couldn't help it.'

I looked at him respectfully. For a time, Dan Rutland had looked a good runner for the World Championship stakes. He'd had a tough break. Now it seemed like he was a back number. That's the way it is with the fight game; you're either hauling yourself up the ladder to the top and you've got plenty to gain … or, if you get knocked off the ladder on the way up, you get no sympathy and nobody comes around you wanting to help.

The train was just about to leave the Junction. The cops and Miller and everyone else had decided June Miller, without a doubt, was somewhere way back down the track.

I shook Ugly-puss's hand. 'Best of luck, fella.'

Miller, who was surrounded by officials, yelled: 'Rutland, you worthless hunk, there's work to do.'

Rutland took that. He let that pompous little idiot bawl him out that way. He said huskily, 'So long, fella,' and turned away. As the train began to move, I saw Ugly-puss bend down and pick up Miller's luggage and trail forlornly across the platform behind the horde of officials.

6

We hit Mason City at about six in the evening. I was off the train as soon as it stopped, and waiting outside the station with a taxi by the time the pallbearers appeared and pushed the flower-laden casket into a waiting hearse.

The hearse drove slowly, and I followed behind in the taxi, keeping about two hundred yards between us.

Mason City was very much a mid-Western town. The centre of the city was constructed mainly of bricks and cement, but out toward the suburbs the traditional timber built villas became more numerous.

Taylor lived about twenty minutes from the centre of the town. His brightly-painted villa was neatly concealed by a ring of cedar trees.

I watched the hearse turn off into the gateway and instructed my driver to carry on down the road.

After a time, I told him to turn around and draw into the kerb, and then I sat there smoking until the empty hearse swung out from the drive again and headed off toward town.

We started off again, and as we passed Taylor's villa I memorised every detail of it, so that I should know it again.

Then I told the driver to take me back to the city.

I went into a telephone booth, looked up 'Private Investigators' and made a note of the three private eyes who were in the vicinity.

The first place I called at was the kind of place I was looking for. It was situated on the third floor of an unkempt, very dirty, block of offices.

As I walked in, a shirt-sleeved janitor with an eye-patch looked up from his racing sheet and then looked away again.

I climbed up the uncarpeted, creaking stairs, and my hand ran along the banister rail, collecting the dirt and grease of weeks. There was the pungent odour of cats and stale tobacco smoke.

D J Evans rented two very small rooms. The outer room housed a pimply-faced girl with a snub nose and dark greasy hair. When I came in, she looked up over the top of a pulp magazine and raised one eyebrow enquiringly. I noticed that her finger nails were dirty and that the varnish was chipped off them.

I said: 'Will you tell Mr Evans that Mr Janson wants see him?'

She chewed gum owlishly, and her cow-like eyes indicated she was trying to decide whether I was worth being polite to or not. She decided to compromise, thrust the magazine in a desk drawer, hitched her stocking through her frock and got up.

'I'll see if he'll see you,' she said.

She went through the door leading to what was

obviously Mr D J Evans's sanctum, and closed it carefully behind her. I looked around me. The windows were dirty, hadn't been cleaned in months; dust lay on files that obviously hadn't been used; dirty coffee cups and a blackened kettle stood near a gas ring over in one corner of the room; and the carpet was frayed and puffs of dust came up when I tapped it with my toe.

This was no private investigator's office. This was the office of a man who scratched a living lying under hotel beds providing evidence for divorce.

But Mr Evans was going to be just the kind of man I wanted to meet. He'd have his ear to the ground ready and waiting for every tit-bit of local gossip. He'd earn a few nickels by obtaining information that no decent fellow would ever talk about, spy on employees, prostitute his soul for a buck, and probably wasn't above a little blackmail as a sideline.

About five minutes passed before the door opened and the girl came out. She looked flushed, and a wisp of her hair had fallen across her forehead. I guessed that she and Evans had been busy cleaning up his office, just on the off-chance that I might be an important client.

'Mr. Evans will see you now,' she said, and stood on one side, holding the door open for me.

I pushed past her, and a short, ferrety-eyed man with high, bony cheekbones and a sharp, pinched nose worked up a grin of welcome and held out his hand, upon which were two highly ornate rings.

'I'm pleased to meetcher, Mr Janson,' he said.

'Yeah.' I turned and looked pointedly at the office girl who, in an effort to look business-like, had produced a note-pad and pencil

'My secretary,' he explained. 'She is fully conversant with all my business.'

'This is private,' I said heavily.

It looked like he was going to say that this was all right and everything would be in confidence and so on, and so on, and then he caught my eye.

'You'd better leave us, Joa– ... Miss Kaye,' he hastily corrected himself.

She stared at him angrily, tossed her head, and slammed the door behind her with such force that the key fell on the floor.

Evans ran a finger around his collar, and looked at me uneasily. He was wondering what I was thinking.

Hell! What did I care? He wasn't the first guy to be under the thumb of his secretary, and he wouldn't be the last, either.

I came to the point quickly. 'Mr Evans,' I said, 'I want information, and I'm prepared to pay for it.'

There was a greedy gleam in his eye as he reached for his note pad. 'I think you'll find that we give good service, Mr Janson.'

'I don't want service, I want information.'

He looked at me calculatingly. 'What information?' he asked.

'Information about two people. I want the whole works. Right from the day they were born, up to what they had for breakfast this morning.'

He said briskly: 'A routine investigation.'

'No, I want more than that. I want the whole story, and most especially I want the dirt. As much dirt as you can dig up.'

'I see,' he mused. He drummed his fingers

thoughtfully on the desk. 'You're interested in politics, I take it ?'

'Look fella! I'm not answering questions. I'm asking them. Can you get me what I want?'

'For twenty bucks a day and expenses. I'll get anything you want.'

'I'll pay you a hundred bucks if I can have the information tomorrow.'

He realised I meant business, and a hundred bucks sounded good to him. He said crisply: 'I want an advance.'

I dropped two ten-spots on the desk in front of him. 'You'll get the other eighty when I get the information.'

He snatched up the two bills and thrust them into his pocket quickly, and threw a glance at the door as though he was scared his secretary might see him doing it. I said: 'The names of the two fellas are T A Taylor, of Thornvale, Derwent Avenue, and Dr Spiller, of Rosemead, Tralawney Park.'

He wrote the names slowly on the page in front of him, and I could see the muscles at the side of his temples contracting spasmodically. I took a chance and said: 'I came to you because I knew you'd be likely to know about them.'

He looked at me broodingly. 'Who said that?' he demanded.

I got up leisurely. 'I'll be around tomorrow,' I said. 'Better have that information ready for me if you want that eighty bucks!'

'You'll have it,' he promised.

When I went out, the secretary was engrossed in her magazine again. She glared at me, and her eyes bored into the back of my neck. When I got to the outer door, I turned and stared back, and then allowed my eyes to drop to where her legs showed beneath the desk top. I kept staring until she got all hot and bothered, and when I shut the door behind me, she was doubled up trying to find out what was wrong with her legs.

The newsboys were on the streets, and June Miller's disappearance was hitting the headlines. I bought a paper, went into a drug store, ordered a cup of coffee, and brought myself up to date with what was happening.

It seemed that June Miller had done the complete disappearing act. Every mile of track between Clork Junction and Des Moines had been gone over, and there wasn't a trace of June, not even the combings of her hair or a piece of her skin. She had disappeared from a train travelling at sixty miles an hour as completely as though she had slipped into another dimension of which this world had no conception.

Millionaire Miller, always conscious of his wealth, had started the whole of Iowa on a manhunt by offering twenty grand to anyone offering information that might lead to finding June.

There was even a bit about Dan Rutland being the bodyguard and being discharged by Miller for gross neglect of his duty.

I stirred my coffee thoughtfully. Anything was likely to happen within the next twenty-four hours. I was going to break into Taylor's house and inspect that casket. I'd mixed it with those pallbearers already, and there were too many of them for me. A fella like Ugly-puss could prove to be useful to me.

I borrowed a piece of paper and a pencil from

the store hop and roughed out a brief cable inviting Ugly-puss to join me at Mason City if he'd like a few days' work. I gave my address as the hotel I could see opposite through the drug store window.

I sent off the cable, booked a room for myself at the hotel, and spent the rest of the evening eating a solitary dinner, drinking Scotch and figuring out all kinds of ways in which it might be possible to get out of trouble if Uncle Taylor or somebody found me breaking in.

Around about one o'clock in the morning, I got the commissionaire to find me a cab, and off I went to Thornvale.

7

I got out of the taxi some quarter of a mile away from the Taylors' home and walked the rest of the way. Folks in these parts were suburban and went to bed early, and presumably got up early. I didn't meet anybody on the way, and I didn't see more than one house lighted up

When I got to the Taylors' drive, the moon had edged behind a cloud, and if anybody had been looking out of the window, the chances were I would not have been spotted.

I followed along the drive, walking on the grass verge, until I got close to the house, and then I skirted off around to the rear, trampling down a coupla flower beds and narrowly missing falling into an ornamental pond.

I'd figured it this way: the casket was sure to be on the ground floor somewhere, because it was a heavy thing to pull up and down the stairs.

It was pretty certain that there were French windows looking out on to the grounds at the back of the house, and provided you have a glass cutter, French windows are just about the easiest things to open.

My guess was right: they were French windows. I lurked in the shadows for half an hour or more, making sure that there was nobody around, and then I slipped up close to the house.

I had some brown paper and a tube of glue in my pocket. I smothered the brown paper in glue, pressed it hard against the French window just above where the door handle should be, and got out my glass cutter. There was a piece of string I'd attached to the brown paper, and I held this with my left hand while I described a circle with the glass cutter around the brown paper.

It was a good cutter, fitted with a diamond. It cut the glass like wire going through cheese. I tapped the brown paper gently, and it fell inwards with the glass. Holding on to the string the way I was prevented the glass from falling inside, smashing on the floor and maybe arousing the household.

After that, I got my arm inside the hole I'd cut, felt around for the door handle and then carefully let myself in. There was just one faint squeak from the hinges and that was all.

I breathed a sigh of relief. So far, so good. I unclipped my breast pocket pencil torch and flicked it around the room. It was a kind of a sun-parlour with cane chairs and tables, and a ping-pong table. That wasn't so good. I'd had the faint hope that I'd be lucky enough to hit the room containing the casket first go off. As it was, it looked like I'd have to do a little exploring.

I left the French window open, slipped off my shoes and placed them just at the entrance to the door. There was no telling when I might have to make a quick exit, and I didn't want to fumble opening doors when a few seconds might save me from a few weeks in gaol on a charge of housebreaking.

I crossed to the far door, turned the handle softly,

and found myself in the corridor. I stood still for a moment, listening. There was no sound from any part of the house.

There were three other doors leading off the corridor and any one of these might contain the casket or a sleeping man who would be awakened by me.

Well I was taking my chances being here, wasn't I? I took the nearest door on my left, and opened it gingerly. When I shone my torch around, I caught a glimpse of an old dining table lined with straight-backed chairs.

That left two more doors to choose from. Again I took the nearest, and this time I was lucky. I knew it as soon as I opened the door. There was the sweet, sickening smell of flowers that are already beginning to die.

I slipped inside, being careful to leave the door slightly open in case I needed to exit in a hurry, and used my torch.

There were flowers everywhere, hanging on the walls, draped over the mantelpiece, and piled up in the windows. Strangely enough, there weren't any on the casket, which was mounted on trestles in the middle of the room.

I went over to it and inspected it. It was ornate and expensive, and all told there were about a dozen screws to hold down the lid. I got out my three-in-one screwdriver, fitted it together, and began to use it.

That was when I got my first surprise. Only four of those screws were holding the lid in position The other eight were dummies. The hair began to creep on the nape of my neck. I began to wonder what I was going to see. Somewhere in the house a board creaked, and I switched off the torch, and crouched there in the dark, listening intently, and wondering if I had disturbed the other occupants of the house.

After a time, I switched on the torch again and took out the last screw. It turned easily, and when I looked at the screw hole I could see specks of oil in the worm.

Well, this was what I'd come to find out, and now was my moment. I slid back the lid, firmly expecting to find that the casket was stuffed with sand, or earth, or something equally weighty. But there was a queer, hollow feeling in my stomach when first of all I saw silky golden hair piled around a white brow. For the moment, I felt so sick and shaky that I had to stop; my heart was pounding like a trip-hammer.

With an effort, I threw off the feeling of nausea and slid the casket lid down further, past the gently shaped eyebrows, the closed eyes and the pale cheeks of a woman.

I didn't recognise her at first, because beneath her cheekbones the flesh was puckered and pushed out of shape by a dirty rag drawn tightly through her jaws.

All this time subconsciously I'd been dreading that the girl was Sally, but when I finally recognised her as June Miller, I got so excited I almost dropped the torch.

It had never occurred to me that there would be anybody alive in that coffin, and while I stared at her, it gave me a shock to see the vibration of her nostrils.

When I saw that, I didn't wait any longer. I ripped off the lid of the coffin and put it on the floor.

June Miller was a tight fit; her bound hands were scraped where I had pulled back the coffin lid, and little trickles of blood crept through the torn skin. Her blouse had been ripped half off one side of her body, and there were two ugly red blotches, just below the heart, that looked like they might have been made by a hypodermic. That was a reasonable assumption to make, because June Miller was obviously drugged.

I got my hand under her head and half levered her out of the casket. She was heavy, limp and dead to her surroundings.

It was difficult manoeuvring the torch while holding her up and untying the gag at the back of her head. As I was doing it, my foot caught against the casket lid and it fell over with a loud impact against the floor. That scared me. I froze. I must have stood there without moving for about five minutes, straining every nerve, listening so intently I could almost hear the house growing old.

Maybe the noise seemed much louder to me than it actually was; it certainly didn't seem to arouse anyone. I breathed a sigh of relief, got my arm around June Miller and lifted her out of the casket. There wasn't a suitable chair for me to put her in, so I sat her on the floor and propped her up against the wall while I got the cords off her wrists. Then I opened one of her eyes and examined the pupil. It was dilated to a pinpoint. She was drugged all right. She was stuffed to the eyebrows with dope. I felt her heart and, though faint, it was beating quite steadily.

Then I sat in a chair, got out a cigarette and began to think. It was quite clear now what had happened to June Miller f on the train. By some means or another she had been induced to enter the special compartment that had been set aside for the casket, and promptly put to sleep. It wouldn't have taken many moments to take off the casket lid, pop June Miller inside, complete with gag and bound hands in case the drug should not exercise its control long enough, and then replace the lid and the flowers.

It needed a cool mind and great effrontery to pull off a job like that, and secretly I had to admire the efficiency with which June Miller had been hijacked from right under the noses of her father and the cops.

Hijacked wasn't really the word. Snatched was the word. I realised right away that nobody was going to all the trouble of carting around caskets with millionaires' daughters inside unless there was a strong probability that someone was going to have to pay ransom. I thought I knew who that someone would be! And there were still a lot of questions that had to be answered. Had the casket been empty when it was first put on the train? Probably it had, but if so what had happened to Sally, and where was she? Was she alive or dead? And who was behind this daring snatch? And how did he intend to carry it through with all the police in the State of Iowa scouring the countryside and towns, and every citizen trying to earn himself ten thousand bucks.

Then I suddenly sat up with a jerk. Here was I sitting in a house, which I had entered illegally, with a snatched millionaire's daughter on my hands. And like a sap I was sitting down doing a Sherlock Holmes stunt.

My subconscious mind came along and dug me hard in the ribs. 'Hey, fella!' it bawled. 'Don't be a sap. Scram!' I got up, went over to June, and listened to her breathing. I lifted her hand, and when I let it go, it flopped back on to the floor. I didn't know what drug they'd been feeding her, but whatever it was, it looked like she was going to be sleeping for a good long while yet. I bent down, got the upper part of her body across my shoulders and heaved. When I stood up, it felt like she weighed a ton. I'd noticed that before; pick up a dame who wants to be picked up and she'll be as light as a feather. But if you try lifting her when she's unconscious, she'll feel like double the poundage.

I got out into the corridor, fumbled my way towards the sun-parlour, and actually had my hand on the door knob when the lights sprang on in the corridor. I didn't waste a second; I shoved hard at the door and blustered across the room towards the French windows. The lights went on when I got half way there. A couple of the pallbearers were standing in front of the French windows, and a third was standing by the light switch. The one by the light switch was holding a blue Luger in his hands, and it was levelled at the pit of my belly. He said grimly: 'Just drop the dame, buddy, and don't try anything!'

I looked at him and tried to register amazement, and at the same time I tightened my grip on June, and all at once swung her down in front of me. I was surprised the fella with the gun hadn't realised I was going to make this move. He daren't shoot now for fear of killing the millionaire's daughter.

But it wasn't he who was dumb, it was me. And I didn't realise it until about two seconds before it happened. I just sensed someone behind me, sensed movement, heard the air swishing, then my head exploded into a thousand fragments.

8

There were pinpoints of light that might have been stars; they got bigger and then they got smaller, and each time they got bigger they got much bigger than they had ever been before, and then they became so big they fused into one, so that all was light, and I moved my head and a felt a sharp jab of pain skewer through my temples.

The light became grey and slowly became light again, and with a shock I suddenly realised that I was looking at a whitewashed ceiling. I moved my head, and again pain knifed through me and a groan forced itself from my lips

And then a voice that I recognised spoke to me and did things to me.

'Hank,' said the voice. 'Hank, are you all right?' I steeled my nerves against the pain and turned over on my side. As I did so, whatever I was lying on moved, crumbled and dug into my viciously.

Yes, it was Sally, lying there with me, her clothes filthy from the coal, her hands tied behind her back, and her legs doubled up behind her and fastened to her wrists. Tied the way she was, she couldn't move an inch.

But at that moment I didn't care about anything

except that Sally was there, and that she was alive, and that at last I was seeing her again.

Her eyes were full of concern.

'Hank,' she said. 'Tell me, are you all right?'

'I guess so!' I said, and put my hand up to feel my head. At least I tried to do so, but then found that, like Sally, I was doubled up with my wrists and ankles strapped closely together.

She said: 'There's blood all down your face, Hank,' and her voice sounded like she was scared I was going to die.

'That's okay, kid.' I told her. 'Somebody just sapped me; they didn't do much more than break the skin.'

I looked around. We were lying in a large, windowless cellar, illuminated by a single shadeless electric light. I gave a start as I saw Tune Miller lying on the other side of me. She wasn't strapped up like we were. She was still doped. Her breasts were hardly moving as she breathed. I looked back at Sally.

'Where the hell are we, and what's happening?' I asked.

She said: 'We're in the cellar of my home!'

I was beginning to remember now; the pallbearers, the man with the gun, something smashing down at my head. I said: 'Look Sally, what goes on here?'

She began to cry then. Big tears formed at the corners of her eyes and rolled down her cheeks. It got me mad to see her looking miserable that way. 'Sally,' I snapped at her. 'You gotta tell me, what's all this about?'

She sobbed a bit, and then managed to say wildly, 'I don't know Hank, I don't know!'

Her voice sounded shrill, and I knew she was on the point of hysterics. I yelled at her, dominating her, trying by the power in my voice to hold back the hysteria rapidly mounting inside her. 'Sally,' I yelled. 'Stop it, kid! Hold on to yourself! Hold on, damn you!'

My words got home to her. The rigidity of her body slackened, and the mad look died from her eyes. After a while, I said, 'D'you feel better, kid?'

'Yes,' she said, 'I feel better now, Hank.'

'Well enough to tell me things?'

'I … think so.'

'Well, tell it right from the start. Tell it just the way it happened. Right from the time you saw me last.'

She swallowed. 'I'll try!' she said with a plucky little smile.

'Good kid!'

'After I left you,' she began ' I went upstairs to bed. Uncle was already in bed and so was the housekeeper. At about six o'clock the next morning, Uncle woke me and said there was something very urgent he wanted me to do. He insisted that it was most important. I was to drive to the Pentworth Hotel in Armidan City, register as Miss Gough and wait there until he communicated with me again.'

'Did he say why he wanted you to do it?' I asked.

'No, he just said that it was of vital importance that I did this and that he would explain everything to me later.

'It was about a quarter to seven when I set off, and I arrived at about twelve o'clock. I waited all that day, all the next day, and then during the evening on the third day, Uncle came for me. He told me that everything had worked quite satisfactorily and that we were going home.'

I suddenly remembered. 'Did you tell him that I would be calling for you?' I asked.

'Of course! I left a letter for Uncle to give you.'

'Okay,' I told her, 'Carry on!'

'When we got out to the car, Dr Spiller was sitting in the back, and then we started off for home. Uncle was driving and Dr Spiller was sitting next to me.

'When we were well out of town, Dr Spiller opened his medicine bag and pulled out a hypodermic. We joked about it and he told me that he was getting it ready for a patient of his, and then when it was loaded he suddenly got hold of me and thrust the needle in my arm.

'That's all I know, Hank. I didn't know anything more until I woke up here.'

'I want you to tell me something, Sally. What's the relationship between you and your uncle? Has he got any affection for you?'

'I think so,' she said. 'He's always taken an interest in me.'

'And he's kept you at his own expense ever since your parents died?'

'Well, there's the Trust of course.'

'Trust?' I said quickly, 'You mean your parents left some dough?'

'Oh yes!' she told me. 'Uncle was entitled to the dividends on my parents' estate until I'm twenty-one, and after that the money and the property reverts to me.'

I said grimly: 'There's just one thing I wanna know Sally. What happens to the dough your folks left if you die before you inherit?'

She said simply: 'It goes to Uncle, of course.'

'Yeah!' I said meaningfully. 'That's what I thought.'

I saw the horror flood into her eyes. 'Hank,' she said, 'you don't think … !'

'Yeah!' I said, 'I do!'

We went on talking for a long while after that. I told her all that had happened in Des Moines and on the train, and slowly but surely missing parts of the story began to become clear.

Should Sally die, there was about fifty thousand dollars that would go to her Uncle. That wasn't peanuts! It seemed a nice scheme that Sally should appear to die, because then her Uncle would obtain her inheritance.

What complicated the issue was the Miller snatch being introduced at the same time. It was beginning to look like Dr Spiller and Uncle Taylor were two very smart guys trying to pull off a snatch and an inheritance at the same time.

'Bui what will happen to June?' Sally asked me.

'That's easy! I can tell you the answer to that! Father Miller is going to receive a letter offering his daughter in return for a few hundred thousand bucks. If he don't pay out, the next time he sees his daughter she'll be in the morgue!'

Sally was horrified. 'I don't believe it!' she said. 'Uncle Taylor wouldn't do anything like that!'

'About this Doc Spiller,' I said. 'How long has he known your Uncle?'

'About a year,' she said. 'He met Uncle through business.'

'And they've been seeing more and more of each other,' I suggested.

'Yes,' she said, 'that's right. How did you know?'

A knob of coal was digging into my left hip, and red-hot burning pains were searing my wrists where the cords cut into me. By jerking my body, I was able to get into a more comfortable position.

'You gotta be sensible, Sally,' I told her. 'You gotta

get this into your head. Your uncle and Dr Spiller are trying to pull something together. My guess is that Dr Spiller is the brains and your uncle is only the cat's paw, but you gotta realise, Sally, they're both in this right up to their necks.'

She looked terrible. I felt sorry for the kid. 'I can't believe it!' she said over and over again. 'I can't believe Uncle would do anything like this!'

'Dr Spiller's a smart guy,' I told her. 'Maybe he's got the finger on your uncle for something or other.'

We were interrupted then because the cellar door opened, and in came a couple of the pallbearers and the two men we had been talking about.

The first thing Spiller did was to go over to June Miller, pull back her eyelid, take her pulse and then fumble in his bag. Without a word, he jabbed the hypodermic into the soft skin below her bared breast and squeezed home the plunger.

Uncle Taylor was standing in the doorway, his hands shaking and his eyes twitching. He was trying not to look at Sally, and he was trying not to look at me. He was trying not to look at June Miller, and in fact he was trying not to look at anything. If there'd been a nice big heap of sand around he could have stuck his head into, he'd have been happy.

Sally cried out to him:

'Uncle!' she said. 'Uncle! These ropes are hurting me. Let me go, please, please!'

Taylor tried to make out he hadn't heard her, and Dr Spiller, who had just finished with June, got up and said tersely: 'Cut on that whining, Sally!'

I figured I had a right to be asking some questions and making some demands also. I said loudly: 'Hey you lousy bums, if you don't undo these ropes, I'm goin' to start gettin' tough and take you apart!'

One of the pallbearers cat-footed over to me and swung his foot at my head. He intended that my nose should be spread over my face, but I dug my chin into my chest and took the force of the blow on my forehead.

'Shut yer trap!' he yelled.

Maybe if I hadn't had my feet tied, or my hands tied, and maybe if there'd been only one of them instead of four, and if I hadn't got a split head that was still bleeding, I'd have felt like being a big hero and bawling them out. But as things were, and being a very sensible guy sometimes, I buttoned up and let my ears flap instead.

Dr Spiller looked at me calculatingly. 'You've gone to an awful lot of trouble to get yourself into difficulties,' he said.

I glared up at him. He said slowly: 'We've put a lot of thought and initiative into our plans, and you've caused us a lot of trouble.'

'I'm pleased to hear it!' I told him.

I got a kick in the pit of the belly for that, and tied up the way I was, I couldn't even double up in pain. When I came to the surface of consciousness again, Spiller was re-charging his hypodermic. In his hands it looked a pretty ugly weapon. He went back to June, opened her eyelid again, smacked her face hard a number of times with the flat of his hand and then snapped at one of the pallbearers: 'Get a chair, quick.'

I saw a tremor run through June. It was like a tiny ripple spreading across an immense millpond. Dr Spiller took her head between his hands and revolved it around on her shoulders. She moaned slightly. It was little more than a rasping breath.

One of the pallbearers got back with the chair.

They lifted June on to the chair, and she slumped there with one of them standing behind her, holding her shoulders to stop her falling sideways.

She didn't look very much like the glamorous girl I'd seen at Des Moines. Her white skirt was torn and creased and filthy with coal dust. Her long legs were dirty and scratched, and her white blouse was nothing but a dirty rag, half-torn from her body. Maybe with a good clean-up and a new set of clothes she'd have looked the goods again. Right now she didn't do anything more than arouse compassion.

Dr Spiller kept slapping her face hard. Her cheeks began to flame with the imprint of his fingers. June groaned again some more, and this time her eyelids flickered.

'She'll be around in a minute,' said the doctor. He stood back and watched June broodingly He said: 'Got that paper, Taylor?'

Uncle Taylor gave a nervous start. His hands fluttered, fumbling in his pocket.

'Bring it here,' said Spiller.

Taylor stumbled over to him, his face working and fingers trembling Dr Spiller looked at him contemptuously.

'Pull yourself together, man,' he rapped.

Uncle said, quaveringly: 'I don't like it, Spiller. I wish to hell we'd never started this. It's too big.'

Dr Spiller's face changed His lips set in a thin, straight line and his eyes seemed to burn into Uncle so that he flinched away. Spiller said very, very slowly: 'I'm beginning to think your usefulness is coming to an end.'

Uncle's white hand fluttered to his mouth. 'No,' he said, horror stricken. 'No. Don't do anything.'

Dr Spiller bared his teeth in a grimace of disgust,

then turned back to June, whose eyes had opened. She looked around, her eyes dumb, uncomprehending.

Dr Spiller thrust a pen in her hand. 'Sign this,' he ordered.

June stared at the pen as though she didn't know what it was. She raised her hand to her forehead, but the fella behind grabbed her wrist and pulled her hand to her side again.

Dr Spiller slapped her face hard. 'Sign this paper,' he said again.

The pain of the blow brought a gleam of consciousness into her drugged mind.

'You hurt,' she whined.

Dr Spiller slapped again, really hard. June shrieked.

'Sign this,' he insisted.

June was making a great effort now. She stared at the printed note, her eyes reading the words and her mind trying to make sense of them And slowly she did understand. Her eyes became terror stricken. She looked up at Spiller. She said: 'You've kidnapped me.'

Spiller nodded his head. 'You're a very valuable piece,' he said.

'But that's fantastic. Five hundred thousand dollars.'

'I'll worry about that, you just sign the form.'

She looked at the note again. 'Father will never pay,' she said.

'I'll take care of that. Just sign the note.'

June held out the pen like she wanted Spiller to take it back. 'I'm not going to sign anything,' she said firmly.

Dr Spiller looked at her calculatingly. 'I ain't gonna like hurting you,' he said. 'It'll be better if you sign now without any trouble.'

'I won't sign,' she insisted, and it was amazing how quickly she was recovering her self-confidence.

Spiller shrugged his shoulders. Then he looked at the man standing behind June. 'Hold her, Lane,' he said.

Lane grabbed June's wrists and twisted them around the back of the chair. She struggled, but Lane twisted her wrists viciously, and with a sudden sob of pain she ceased struggling.

Dr Spiller said to the other pallbearer: 'Bare her foot, Daker.'

The other fella approached June warily. She tried to kick out at him, but he dodged around her, spread his bulk on her lap and took one of her legs. He was a strong fella and his hands were large and hairy. As he gripped her ankle and pulled off her shoe, I could almost see her flesh bruising beneath his fingers.

'Better hold her tight,' said Spiller. 'She's likely to jump around a bit.'

He took a cigarette lighter from his pocket, thumbed it into life and held it beneath the sole of June's foot. For a second it was like she wasn't feeling anything. The flame played on the flesh and the skin blackened with smoke and her foot arched. But that was only for a second. After that she screamed, and the horror and pain of that scream screeched through my nerve centres like I was feeling the pain myself.

Daker was a big man. He wasn't the kinda fella I should have liked to carry around. Yet big though he was, in the strength of her agony, June's body turned and squirmed so that he half fell off her lap. He lost his grip on her leg, and it jack-knifed spasmodically, and I could see the muscles jerking and contorting all the way up her leg.

'Hold her, you fools,' growled Dr Spiller.

They held her. It needed both of them, and it was some moments before she was sitting there without struggling, moaning and sobbing with pain.

Spiller said: 'Are you going to sign?'

She acted like she didn't hear him, giving out long sobs of agony.

Dr Spiller nodded at Daker, and the fella grabbed June's leg again. She screamed then like she was going mad.

Dr Spiller said: 'Are you going to sign?'

'Yes,' she screamed. 'I'll sign. I'll sign. For Chrissakes don't do it again. Don't do it.'

Spiller waited a few moments until she got calmer, and then handed her the note and a pen. 'Sign it with your usual signature so your father will know it's signed by you.'

She didn't look up. She grabbed the pen and signed quickly.

Dr Spiller took the note, looked at it carefully, folded it and then put it into his bill-fold. Then he looked at June and said: 'Maybe that ain't your real signature.'

'Why shouldn't it be?'

'Maybe you don't want your Pa to cough up that dough.'

'He will,' she said. 'He'll have to, because I can't stand this much longer.'

'I'll give him further proof, however,' said Spiller, and an idea was gleaming in his eyes.

'The signature's genuine.'

''Maybe I could send him your ear,' said Dr Spiller slowly.

She shrank back as far away from him as she could. There was terror in her eyes now.

'It wouldn't even be painful,' said Spiller methodically. 'A local anaesthetic to freeze the nerves. It'd be off in a second.'

June looked like she was going crazy. It took Daker and Lane all their time to hold her. Her body arched as she strained to get free, and all the time she screamed and screamed. It looked like she was never gonna stop.

Dr Spiller picked up his hypodermic. While the others held her, he pinched the skin beneath her breast into a pucker. The needle slid into the skin, and his thumb pressed hard on the plunger. She went on screaming and struggling for about a minute, and then quite suddenly she slumped. She went right cold. Whatever drug he was using, it musta had a kick like a horse.

Spiller began to fumble in his bag. Lane said quietly: 'Listen, Doc. Ear slicing's a pretty serious business. Her father's gonna yell blue murder if she gets home all cut up. Things like that can get a father mad He may start almost anything then.'

It was on the tip of Spiller's tongue to blast hell outta Lane. But there was something in what the man said. When a dame who's been snatched comes home to daddy safe and sound, he's liable to be so happy at her return and so scared she may get snatched again that he'll want no further trouble.

But if the dame comes home minus an ear, daddy is liable to feel that she's been mutilated for life and somebody's gotta pay dearly for doing it.

Spiller said thoughtfully: 'Maybe you're right there. But we'll send something!' He snapped his fingers. 'I'll tell you what. We'll cut off her hair and send that. Hair can grow again.'

Uncle Taylor had been watching everything that

had happened, with his face working like it was made of elastic. Now suddenly he began to sob like a child.

Spiller shot a quick look at him. 'Get him upstairs and locked in his room,' he told Lane. 'We'd better deal with him later.'

Uncle Taylor suddenly ran from the cellar. Lane plunged after him. We could hear their footsteps on the wooden steps leading upstairs.

Spiller dived down into his bag. Then he walked across to June. His shoulders blocked my vision. But I could hear the snip of the scissors. He was cutting for a long while, and Daker seemed to be helping him. Sally was watching him with horror-filled eyes.

When at last he turned around, his hands were full of the soft, honey-coloured hair that had belonged to June. I glanced at her, and my guts turned over. Dr Spiller had cropped all her hair off, right down to the scalp. It was terrifying, frightening to see her. Her head seemed enormous, and the little irregular tufts of hair about a quarter of an inch in length that sprouted all over her head gave me a weird feeling that I was watching something dreadfully obscene.

It was amazing seeing her almost bald that way. I'd have never believed she was the same girl. Somehow her face seemed to have changed and got out of proportion. Her eyebrows were just ugly exclamation marks drawing attention to the plainness of her features.

I glanced at Sally and saw her shuddering. She was feeling the same as me. June looked revolting. Just to look at her made me feel sick.

I watched Dr Spiller carefully wrap up the hair in brown paper. I said to him: 'D'ya really think you're gonna get away with this?'

He seemed in a better mood now that he'd got the

note signed by June ready to send off together with the hair, the living proof that June was in his hands.

'Of course I'm going to get away with it,' he said. 'Despite your interference.'

'You're gonna have a lotta grief coming to you.'

'If that's the case, you need not worry that it'll bother you. You'll not be around to interfere.'

I narrowed my eyes. He was talking calmly, but there was no denying the threat in his voice.

'In fact, you're gonna have quite a massacre,' I said.

'Not necessarily, not necessarily.'

'Listen, Doc. If you think me and Sally are gonna forget what's happened here, you must be crazy.'

His attitude suddenly changed. His eyes flared at me and I thought I caught at the back of them a gleam of madness.

'I didn't ask you to interfere with my plans. But since you've seen fit to interfere, you must take the consequences.'

'You'll never get away with it.'

I stung his vanity. He wanted to let me see how clever he was.

'You,' he said, 'are going to die. And you're going to die tomorrow morning.'

He scared me the way he said it. He said it like he meant it. But I wasn't gonna let him see I was scared. I said: 'I don't die easy.'

'You're right,' he said. 'You won't die easy. You'll die slowly. Very slowly. You're gonna be buried alive.'

Sally gave a gasp of horror, and I didn't feel very happy either. I saw in a flash what was in his mind. And he carried on talking, confirming what I dimly suspected.

'You saw fit to interfere with my plans. If you had not arrived here, Sally would have been buried tomorrow, as it had originally been intended.'

'You swine,' I mouthed at him. 'You murdering bloody swine.'

He seemed to take that as a compliment. 'You have a quick mind,' he said. 'You realise how everything was planned.'

'Yeah,' I said. 'You and that frightened Uncle bury Sally and grab her inheritance.'

'Precisely,' he said. 'But since you have insisted on interfering, and since something must be done with you, I'm afraid that you'll be buried instead of Sally. Your body will have to be disposed of somewhere.'

'And you'll cut Sally up in little pieces and flush her down the drain, I suppose,' I said.

'Sally will create a problem,' he agreed. 'I'll have to think about that. But you're troublesome, and the sooner we dispose of you the better.'

I said: 'I'm gonna tell you something, Doc. You're crazy. You're a doctor, give yourself some tests. I'm telling you, you're crazy. You wouldn't try this if you weren't.'

I got him on the raw than. And as his eyes flamed at me again, I caught that mad spark gleaming far back behind them. 'You fool,' he mouthed. 'You call me mad. You insult me. And for that I'll make you suffer.'

'See what I mean. You're crazy.'

His eyes burned like live coals, and a vein stood out at the side of his temple and pulsed.

'I'll make you suffer,' he said. 'I was gonna bury you under the influence of drugs. But now you'll be buried … alive You'll feel yourself dropped down into the earth, you'll hear the ropes slip off the coffin. You'll feel through your wooden shell the impact as the first spadeful of earth hits the lid of the coffin. And then the damp thud as more and more earth comes down on top of you. You'll be in darkness, unable to move, and slowly the air will run out and you'll be suffocated. You'll want to scream and pound on the coffin and tear yourself loose, but you'll find it impossible to move, and then … and then … you'll go mad. Do you hear what I say? You'll go mad. Mad. MAD! It'll be you that's mad … not me!'

Sally turned her head away with a sob of terror. I began to struggle desperately with the ropes binding my wrists and ankles. Daker came across and shoved his foot in my guts. 'Quit that,' he yelled.

Spiller fumbled in his bag again while I blinked the tears of pain from my eyes. He said, 'He's gonna be trouble. We'd better give him a dose.' He was measuring phials of liquid, emptying them into the hypodermic. I began to struggle with desperation as he moved in towards me. Sally began to scream. Daker ripped off ray necktie and bared my chest. Spiller jabbed hard with the needle. He jabbed so hard I heard it penetrate the flesh and grate against a rib. It was painful. I sweated as I exerted every ounce of my strength to snap the ropes binding me. It was funny the way it happened. I was straining in desperation at the ropes, Spiller was watching me as though I were a specimen of some kind, Sally was sobbing and Daker looked like he was trying to decide whether to boot my face in or crush my intestines. And then there was nothing.

That's just the way it was. Everything going on and then … nothing.

9

If you look up the word 'claustrophobia' in the dictionary, it will be described as *an excessive dislike of confined spaces.*

That is what I consider a masterpiece of understatement.

If at any time you happen to wake up in the dark and know beyond a shadow of doubt that you're crammed into a coffin that's gonna be shoved into the earth at any minute, think over how you feel and see if you would simply say that you have an excessive dislike of confined spaces.

Brother, I nearly went stark raving mad the moment I realised where I was. Nothing had happened yet, as far as I knew. But just being in the coffin was enough to make me nearly burst those thousands of blood vessels that entwine around the brain.

I guess I probably was really insane for some minutes. But there's a difference between a sane man and a fella who's really crazy. We're all liable to blow our top at some time. We're all liable to get overstrained by badly strung emotions, and we're all liable, even if it's for only a few seconds, to feel and know that we're actually crazy for those few seconds.

Now the fella that's not crazy can take care of those rare, unguarded moments when he is crazy for a few seconds. That part of his mind that is logical and thinking comes to the front and rescues him. That part of the mind comes to the fore and says: *You won't get any place this way. You gotta use your intelligence.*

It's useful to have the sensible and logical part of your brain around. You'd better pray, fella, that every time you blow your top for a few seconds, the conscious part of your mind does step in and take a part. Because if it doesn't, fella, you've had it. You're really crazy and for all time.

My logical senses were working okay. There were those seconds or minutes of blind, fear-stricken insanity, during which time I was reduced to blind, senseless, animal feelings engulfed in a vortex of unfeeling exhilaration. That was the mind's escape from the horror it was faced with.

If things had worked out differently, if I had wound up under the ground, it would have been better for me to have remained insane. Maybe it was a bit heartless of my logical mind to jerk me back into sanity when there was a very good chance I was gonna suffer intense physical agony. But I'm the kinda guy that never gives up.

When my mind cleared, when the red haze had evaporated, I stared into the darkness and tried to move. It was like I was packed in a sardine tin. I couldn't move one part of my body. Even my fingers were wadded up. I knew what had been done. While drugged, I'd been thrust into the casket, and rags and other things had been wadded over me and around me. When the lid was on the casket, there wasn't a thing I could do. It was like being buried in cement.

Even my mouth and jawbone wouldn't move, because of the stuff firmly wadded around them. I couldn't shout either, because there was a gag in my mouth that was choking me. The wonder was that I could breathe at all.

My logical self reasoned that I couldn't be buried yet because, if so, I'd never have recovered consciousness. I'd have died when my air was cut off by six feet of earth or more piled on top of me.

I also reasoned that there must be air holes of some kind somewhere in the casket, otherwise June would never have survived the journey from Des Moines. The way I was wadded up and packed in, though, probably meant that at the most it was only a thin trickle of air, barely enough to keep me alive. The next thing I thought of was escape. The lid was the only means of escape, and I tried to brace my body and force upwards. But the way I was lying didn't permit me to do very much bracing, and I remembered that the lid slid on to the casket rather like the lid of a pencil box. I had as much chance of pushing that off as I had of pushing out the sides. In short, I had no chance.

The hope was that at some time during the burial ceremony I'd have the opportunity to attract somebody's attention to the casket in some way.

But right then I couldn't figure out any way that might be possible.

And then, one of my senses came into play. I could hear! I couldn't hear much. It was like being in a telephone box and trying to listen to what went on outside. I could get only the gentle vibrations and sounds that were very loud.

But I knew that somebody was doing something to

the casket. I could hear that quite distinctly. And it didn't take long to realise that it was a screwing sound I could hear.

My heart jumped. I wanted to know if it was a screwing down or unscrewing I could hear. One meant extinction, the other meant hope.

It was an interminable age waiting like that. I thought the screwing would never come to an end. But it did. And then, after a pause, there was a scraping noise and I felt soft movement all over me. That was because the casket lid was being slid open.

It slid back just so my eyes could see out. I blinked in the bright light, blinked into the crazed eyes of Dr Spiller.

'Ah,' he breathed. 'You're conscious.'

I tried to tell him with my eyes what I thought of him. I'm told eyes can speak volumes. I let off a coupla volumes in as many seconds. That was all I could do.

He grinned. 'I'm pleased to see you've recovered consciousness. I so much want you to know what's happening. There's been a change of plan. You're not to be buried after all.'

He musta seen the flash of hope in my eyes. He grinned with pleasure.

'Burying would be dangerous,' he explained. 'There's such a thing as exhumation. We couldn't risk that. So, my dear friend, you're going to be cremated instead.'

If I could have moved, I'd have shuddered with horror.

He was delighted at the torment I was suffering. He said: 'The hearse is arriving in half an hour. There's the journey, of course, and then the service. I should think probably … yes, you've got about an hour before the flames begin to lick around you. Of course, you won't burn so much as roast. It'll probably be some minutes of intense heat before the flames get through to you. Your blood will probably boil in your veins, and for the few brief seconds that you still live you'll suffer the torments of all hell.'

All I could do was to stare at him, trying to ask a question with my eyes. He was smart. He understood.

'You want to know about Sally? If I'm right, shut one eye.'

I shut one eye.

I could tell from his eyes that he was on the brink of madness, and his madness took the form of imposing pain upon other people. He rejoiced in what he intended to do to Sally, and he revelled in telling me and seeing the pain in my eyes.

'I have decided,' he said, 'that Sally shall be buried in the coal cellar. Bricking-in will be the precise method I shall adopt. You will probably recall the story of Edgar Allen Poe dealing with such a situation.'

I felt sick. I remembered the story clearly enough. It was about somebody being bricked up in a cellar. The story described the agonies experienced as the bricks mounted higher and higher and the supply of air became less and less until it was finally cut off, leaving the man to darkness and to death.

'You'll have something to think about until ...' said Spiller.

He shut the lid then. It slid over my eyes and smoothly clicked into position. The screwing began again, and this time I knew they were going home into place with the finality of death.

The next half-hour seemed to slip by. It seemed no time before I heard muffled noises, felt swaying and knew the casket was being lifted and carried.

I strained my ears, dreading everything I heard, yet insisting on knowing everything.

The casket suddenly slid forward and stopped as it hit something.

In my mind's eye I could see all that had happened. The casket being carried out to the hearse by the bare-headed, solemn-faced pallbearers, Daker and Lane probably taking the front of the casket. I saw the end of the casket rested on the runners in the hearse, the casket sliding forward and hitting the stops.

I listened intently and heard the doors close a long, long way away.

Shortly after, a soft vibration began. Nothing I could hear, but a faint vibration that affected all of the casket. That was the hearse engine. We were probably rolling along now toward the crematorium.

It was at this point that I began to pray for insensibility, insanity or anything else that would let me forget everything that was happening until it was all over.

Think it over. How would you feel, wadded down in a casket, on the way to the crematorium and incineration, lying there able to know exactly what was happening about you, with maybe hundreds of people watching, and yet being powerless to make the slightest move that would bring them to your help.

I prayed for insensibility. It didn't come. I prayed for insanity. I tried to drive myself crazy by working up a mad fit of fear. But that didn't work either. And when the vibration stopped and I knew the hearse had reached the crematorium, instead of going into a sweaty-crazed state of mind, I slumped into an ice-cold, calmly reasoning state of mind that was able to weigh up soundly every particle of the approaching horror I was shortly to endure.

The casket slid on the rollers again. And I could see in my mind everything that was happening. The hearse pulling up outside the church. The pallbearers sliding the casket cut from the hearse; the swaying as they carried it shoulder-high through into the chapel; and then the slight jar as they set it down at the far end of the chapel on the wooden runners.

I'd been to cremations. I knew how they worked. The casket was carried into the chapel and placed feet forwards, on a specially constructed table.

The table had wooden rollers, and it was placed against the wall. There was a wooden flap in the wall. The idea was that after the priest had said prayers and blessed the casket and so on, the flap in the wall was opened, the casket was slid along the rollers, through the flap and on to a table the other side of the chapel.

The mourners stayed in the chapel, the flap was closed and the mourners prayed. The other side of the wall was the furnace. As the casket came through on to the roller table, the furnace doors were opened wide. The roller table was slid right up against the furnace, and then with one single heave the casket was shot off the table, straight into the white-hot heart of the furnace. The furnace doors were slammed, electrically created draughts forced the heat up to incredible heights. Minutes later, there'd be nothing left to show of what had once been a beautifully-made casket, and in my case, what had once been a live human being.

That wasn't pretty knowledge to have. I knew where I was. I was on the roller table against the wall. Any time now, the preacher was likely to finish his stuff. It'd be less than a minute then. The flap would open, the casket would shoot through and the flap would close behind me. Maybe jittery, white-faced, trembling fingered Uncle Taylor would suddenly begin to sob. But that would be right and proper. A genuine show of emotion at the loss of his niece. Dr Spiller would probably look very, very serious. And the six pallbearers who had thrown in their lot with Dr Spiller, and were risking electrocution to gain a fortune, would feel easier in their minds as evidence that could fry them was sizzled to nothingness.

It's said that in the last few seconds before a drowning man dies, all his previous life passes before him in a flash. I don't believe it. I wasn't drowning, but I knew I was dying. And nothing like that happened to me. All I could do was to think of the heat of that furnace and wonder how much pain I'd suffer before unconsciousness saved me from the torment.

I kept thinking of what was coming, and then I heard the scraping again, the sliding movement. I sucked in my breath and tried to clench my teeth through the gag. I was sliding from the chapel into the furnace room.

This was it!

10

Most of the time, I hate the sordid, never-ending lust for money that seems to dominate almost everybody I meet. For the sake of a few hundred, or a few thousand, little green bills, men *and* women sometimes do the most incredible things. Half the killings in Chicago are caused on account of certain folk wanting to build up for themselves a nice little pile of greenbacks.

But I'm not gonna deny that there are occasions upon which I'm very pleased to see that the glint of folded dollars is wielding an influence. I felt that way when I persuaded Morrow the mortician to part up with some very valuable information.

And I especially felt that way when the lust for dollars saved me from incineration.

You've probably seen beautifully made caskets being tooled off to the cemetery. Some funerals cost a hell of a lotta dough. And doubtless there are many folk who think it's a crying shame to see beautifully made wooden caskets with brass handles and other trimmings being thrust into the earth and covered up.

Doubtless many folks have thought what a waste

this is. But not many folks are in a position to do anything about it.

But there are some people who can do something about it!

Take time off to figure out how much spare dough a fella could knock up by selling slightly used caskets back to the morticians. Boy, he'd make a fortune. If he had the right connections, the same casket could be sold, inhabited, sold back to the mortician, sold again and again and again, maybe a dozen times, all told. That'd show good dividends.

And who are the folk who are in a position to sell the caskets back to the morticians?

As soon as the casket I was on rolled through from the chapel into the furnace room, the screws were started on. There were two screws being taken out at the same time. I couldn't believe my ears at first. I'd abandoned all hope a long while previously. And my first thought was that maybe Dr Spiller had changed plans, had taken me back to Thornvale and was getting ready to have another gloat over me.

And then I realised that this couldn't be so. Everything I'd experienced in the casket indicated I was really in the furnace room.

And then it hit me. I knew suddenly what was happening. Those fellows in the furnace room were smart guys. They weren't the kinda fellas to let a chance to make good dough slip through their fingers.

They were opening up that casket with all speed. They were gonna tip my body out onto the rollers, run me into the furnace, minus the casket, and stow the casket away some place safe where later on they could sell it back to the morticians.

Yeah, they were smart boys. The way they were

working on those screws showed they'd had plenty of practice. And they had to work quick, too, because in a little while the mourners would be around wanting to grab some ashes to preserve in a pot on their mantelpiece

They were working like madmen. What they had to do was to get that casket hidden away safely and quickly. The body was unimportant to them. It was the casket that was important. The only thing they didn't know was that the body was not dead!

I could almost nave swooned with joy when I realised what was happening. And then, as the last screw came loose, the lid was ripped back and almost in the same movement the casket was tipped over on its side and I rolled out on to the roller table.

I'd been cramped into that casket for hours on end. I had been short of air, my circulation had nearly stopped and I hadn't eaten a thing for probably twenty-four hours. When I rolled outta that casket, I was as weak as a kitten.

I just lay there on the table, trying to make my muscles work, and it was like they had died on me. I made a superhuman effort. I heard my bones creak, and pains shot down my spine as I sat up. The gag was cutting into my mouth cruelly. As I sat up, I raised my hands to get it untied.

The two fellas who'd opened the casket hadn't given a second glance to me. They'd just rolled me out on the table, grabbed the casket and carried it to the far end of the room. When I glanced around to see where they were, they were just pushing the casket into a cupboard, standing it on end.

They turned around, both at the same moment, and began to walk towards me. All their movements were swift and methodical like they'd been doing this all their lives – maybe they had. But this trip they changed course.

They both saw me at the same time. I can imagine how those guys musta felt. For years they'd been performing an illegal action that would probably be described by the legal authorities as grave-robbing. They'd made a good sideline of it But probably, even though it was a daily round to them, right at the back of their minds was an uneasy feeling that the dead would resent their actions.

Can you imagine how they felt, turning around and seeing the corpse sitting up and moving his arms?

They were middle-aged guys and not too bright. You didn't have to be a sensitive kinda guy to take on a job like they had. They just stared at me, their eyes widening and their mouths dropping. One of them went dead white, his eyes glazed, and he just slumped down on his knees. The other went blue. I mean it. I'd never seen anybody look blue like he did. I've heard the tag about a fella being in a blue funk, but I'd never before seen or thought it possible that a human face could go that colour. He stared at me and I stared at him. His eyes bulged so that they seemed like white billiard balls with pupils marked on them. And then his nerve snapped. He started to run. He ran straight at a door leading away from the chapel. He nearly tore off the door handle trying to get that door open, and he didn't wait for the opening to be wide enough for him to get through. He musta scraped a lotta skin off himself on to the door-post and the door-jamb. I've never seen anyone moving so fast. He moved just like he was a streak.

All this takes a long time to describe. But it took

just about fifteen seconds to happen. I was still untying the gag when that fella shot out of the door. But I wasn't worrying about him. I was worrying about Dr Spiller. If these two fellas caused trouble, the chances were Dr Spiller would be warned and get away. I had to silence the guy who was left.

My nerveless fingers managed to get the gag untied. I swung my feet off the table and stood up, shakily. When I walked, I had pins and needles so bad I didn't know I had legs. I made it somehow, bent down and looked at him. He looked like he was out cold for a good long while. But just to make sure, I let him have my fist hard under the jaw. It was a callous way to treat somebody who'd just saved my life. But he didn't do it intentionally and, anyway, he might just as easily have fried me.

Somehow I got over to the cupboard. I knew I'd have to work fast. I got the casket out and half-pulled, half-lifted it over to the furnace. By this time I was in agony. My circulation was restoring itself and I was gasping with pain.

I got the head of the casket over the lip of the furnace. I shoved. The casket moved in about afoot. I shoved again. The white heat blazed out at me, scorching my eyebrows and my hair. I gritted my teeth and shoved and shoved. The other end of the casket was already roaring to ashes in white-hot flames.

I got that casket right inside at the expense of a burned hand. And then I staggered out of the door, sweating from every pore, weak with hunger and my muscles screaming in agony.

But after having come through everything I had, I wasn't gonna give way now.

I got outta that door, out into the open air, into

the grounds behind the furnace. There didn't seem to be anybody around. Blue-face wouldn't be around for a dead cert. The last I'd seen of him, he looked like he was all set for a hundred mile gallop – and without touching the ground, either.

The way I'd left things oughtta keep Dr Spiller happy if anything came out. The casket had been burned and one fella was lying on the ground with a bruise on his jaw. If either of them ever wanted to talk – which I doubted, because they weren't gonna tell the cops they'd been grave robbing – the most that would be thought was that they'd been drunk and one of them had got knocked out.

If Blue-face ever came back, it was pretty safe betting he wasn't gonna talk. Personally, I thought it pretty safe betting he wasn't gonna come back, either.

I walked rapidly across a grass verge, skirted a block of tombstones and got in amongst a bunch of trees. Then I gave myself the once over. I wasn't in bad shape. My clothes were still dirty from the coal, but they looked like good clothes that had got dirty. They didn't look like clothes that had worn dirty. My hands were filthy and I guessed my face musta been grimed with coal dust. But a gents' toilet would put me right.

I ducked out from the trees, making my way steadily in the opposite direction to the chapel, and after passing several large blocks of tombstones and a number of people who stared at me in amazement, I finally reached the confines of the cemetery. There was a brick wall about eight feet high surmounted by glass. I looked up and down. A group of people were gathered around a grave some forty yards further along, and an old woman and an old man were sitting on a seat nearby. Both of them were watching me with undisguised alarm. I took my coat off, rolled it up and spread it over the glass on top of the wall. The old fella opened his mouth. But I reckoned he was so surprised, he couldn't make a noise.

I stepped back a few paces, took a run and leaped. My hands clawed at the top of the wall, my arms flexed, heaving my weight upwards, and then my belly sprawled across the muffled glass. A few moments later, I dropped down the other side of the wall into an avenue lined with cedar trees. I slipped on my jacket and began to walk very fast toward the top of the avenue. I had to get to a gents' toilet and clean myself up before folks began to think I was crazy or something.

11

I found a gents' wash-place, cleaned myself up and grabbed a taxi back to my hotel. I had the feeling that this thing was too big for me to handle by myself. Yet it went against the grain to call in the cops when a good fella like Dan Rutland could do with all those dollar bills millionaire Miller was prepared to push around in exchange for information leading to the return of his daughter.

I didn't wanna see that dough go to the cops. I didn't need it myself. But this was too big for me to handle alone, and Dan Rutland did need that dough!

When I got back to the hotel, I asked the reception clerk:

'Is there anybody asking for me.'

'Sure thing,' he agreed. 'There's a guy named Rutland been hanging around since yesterday waiting to see you.'

'Since yesterday?' I got a queasy kinda feeling in my guts, because I'd thought I'd been around all day yesterday. I was just beginning to realise that I must have been under the effects of that dope for more than twenty-four hours. No wonder I was stiff!

I found Dan in the bar. He was sitting on a high stool with a half-empty glass in front of him looking very miserable.

'Hiya, Dan,' I greeted him.

His eyes lit up and his ugly faced creased in a smile. 'Gee I'm pleased to see ya,' he said. 'I guessed you were a regular guy, but when you didn't show up yesterday I thought ya mighta been giving me the run around.'

'Come on up to my room,' I said. 'I gotta lot to tell ya about.'

I ordered some grub to be sent up to my room and then, as I ate, I told Dan all that had transpired.

'We gotta go to the cops,' he said.

'No, Dan,' I told him. 'We got ourselves a good chance of winding this deal up ourselves. And we gotta work fast. I'm worried about Sally, and she may be in trouble.'

'What do we do?' he asked.

'We're gonna get that Miller girl outta that house and we're gonna get Sally outta that house. Afterwards we can go to the cops with our story and get those swine what they oughtta have coming to them.'

Dan looked dubious. I swallowed the last few mouthfuls, dived under the bed and came out with my grip. I opened it. It contained a six-shooter and an automatic.

'Know how to use this?' I asked Dan.

He hefted the six-shooter 'Sure,' he said. 'I useta do a lotta shooting practice at camp. It keeps your eye in.'

'We ain't got much time,' I told him. 'Dr Spiller will be back from the crematorium pretty soon.'

I rang down and asked the desk to arrange for a hire car to be brought around to the hotel.

I said to Dan: 'Look, this is liable to be tough. There's maybe eight of these eggs to cope with. As far as I know, they're not armed. But they may dig up a few rods from somewhere and there may be some shooting. I don't want to get you into anything you don't want. We can go tell the cops right away if you like.'

Ugly-puss said seriously, 'I guess I oughtta have looked after that dame better. It'll kinda square accounts if I get her outta there myself and turn her over to her pa.'

We had to wait about five minutes for the hire car to be brought around. When it eventually arrived, I climbed into the driving seat and Ugly-puss settled down beside me. It was afternoon and the sun was shining and the roadway shimmered in the heat. But even so, I got cold shivers run down my back when I remembered what had been happening to me that morning. Just by chance, those two furnace men had happened to be interested in getting a little dough ... I stopped thinking about it. It wasn't a pleasant subject and I had a lot to think about where Dr Spiller was concerned.

As we drove along, I told Ugly-puss the layout of Thornvale as I knew it. We also made tentative plans. So when we got within a hundred yards of Thornvale, we drew into the kerb. We walked the rest of the way.

Our plan was to walk in quite calmly if we were seen approaching the house and tell Dr Spiller to release June and Sally, adding that we'd phoned the cops and they were on the way.

But we didn't have to use this plan, which was

rather risky. Nobody had seen us approaching, so we skirted around the lawn and got in through the French windows. The sun parlour was empty, and when we cautiously poked our heads into the corridor, that was deserted, too. At the far end of the corridor was the stairway. The stairs led up and the stairs led down. I jerked my head at Ugly-puss. 'Come on,' I said. 'We'll go for the basement. I'm anxious about Sally.'

It was nerve-wracking making our way along the corridor. We expected any minute that one of the doors would burst open and out would come somebody; Dr Spiller say, or one of the pallbearers.

But we made the top of the stairway without interruption, and as we got there we heard raised voices. I looked at Ugly-puss meaningfully. He nodded. I led the way down the stairs. At the bottom, the corridor was lighted, and a crack of light gleamed from under one of the doors from which came the sound of the voices.

I pussy-footed over to it, glanced over my shoulder to make sure Dan was right behind me. Then with one quick shove I thrust open the door and levelled my gun.

I recognised the place at once as being the cellar in which I'd been imprisoned. But I didn't have much time to notice details. We'd interrupted something that looked pretty mean.

Uncle Taylor was there waving an old six-shooter that was almost as big as himself. I couldn't think how he had the strength to keep it trained on a level with Dr Spiller's belly. But he was managing it somehow. A coupla pallbearers were lined up alongside Dr Spiller. Like him, they had their hands raised above their heads. I didn't blame them for being cautious. The way Uncle Taylor was holding that gun, it looked like it might go off any minute even if they didn't make a false move.

I said: 'All right, uncle, I'll take over now.'

He turned around and gaped at me.

'You can drop that gun,' I said to him, and then one of the pallbearers went into action. He musta been some fella with a gun. I barely saw his hand flick to his pocket. He fired through the pocket twice before my slug caught him in the shoulder. But meantime all hell had broken loose. Uncle Taylor began to fold up. He did it slowly like he was taking his time sitting down in a chair. The other pallbearer went for his gun, and at the same time Uncle Taylor started firing. His first slug wiped out Dr Spiller's face, and the second smashed into his chest. I think the second pallbearer might have got me if it hadn't been for Dan. I could see this man's eyes glaring into mine, and a bullet whined through the doorway an inch from my head. Another slug cut chips from the door. But Dan's heavy six-shooter began to roar. The second pallbearer looked suddenly surprised and then pained. He was still looking that way when his eyes closed and he hit the ground.

There was a lotta smoke around, and in that cellar all those gun shots echoed and re-echoed deafeningly.

But I wasn't worrying about that. I was worrying about Sally. And what I'd seen in the split seconds during the time this action was taking place was enough to get me worried.

The far corner of the cellar had been cleared of coal. A hole had been dug, about two feet square and about six feet deep I guessed. I had reason to think it was about six feet deep, because I could just see the top of Sally's head. She'd been inserted in the hole, and my heart was thumping like a trip-hammer, because I was scared of what had happened to her.

I stumbled across the coal, through the smoke, towards the corner. I tripped over Dr Spiller's leg, which was crooked up, and landed face-down on one of the pallbearers. My hand came down on something wet and sticky.

But I wasn't worrying about any of those things. I clawed my way to the hole. Sally was all right. She looked up at me, and her eyes gleamed with sudden relief.

'Sally,' I breathed. 'Are you all right?'

'I knew you'd come,' she said simply.

'Let's get outta here,' I said. I gave her my hand so I could pull her out, and then for the first time noticed that she was up to her neck in a grey kinda substance. 'Jeezus,' I yelled.

'Get me out, Hank,' she pleaded. 'It's cement. Spiller was gonna cement me in here.'

I felt suddenly faint. Dr Spiller must have been as crazy as a coot.

'It's quick-setting, Hank,' she said, and for the first time I noticed the pain in her voice. Creepers, she musta been suffering hell! Not only was that cement damp and cold and liable to freeze all hell outta her, but at the same time it was sucking at her, drawing the moisture from her body and crushing her with its weight.

'Dan,' I yelled.

He came scrambling over the coals. I didn't need to say anything. I just pointed mutely. We lay down on our chests and began to scoop out the cement with our bare hands. We couldn't have used a shovel, because there wasn't enough room between the sides of the hole and Sally's body. Even as I dug into the cement with my fingernails, I could feel it drying out, hardening. The bottom layers musta been getting pretty near set.

Dan was panting with his efforts, but we didn't seem to be getting no place very quickly. I wiped my hand across my brow. 'We gotta pull her out,' I said.

Dan had got down to one of Sally's armpits. I concentrated on the other side until I'd also scooped away enough cement to get my hands beneath her armpit.

'Ready, Dan?'

He nodded.

We began to heave. I watched Sally anxiously and saw her clench her lips tightly. I was scared. I was scared that the cement had set tight around her hips, and if that had happened, we'd have never got her out without a pickaxe.

'How is it, honey ?' I asked anxiously.

'It's the pressure,' she gasped. 'It's crushing me.'

Dan's face was red with the efforts he was making. I strained hard, my fingers digging into Sally's armpits and my muscles cracking.

There came a slight movement, and I redoubled my efforts. It was like pulling a ten ton wagon. Slowly, slowly, an eighth of an inch at a time, Sally came outta that cement. It sucked at her, clung to her, drew the skin from her body and the clothes from her skin. Tears of pain were welling out of her eyes, but grimly she clenched her teeth and not one sound did the let out.

When her hips got clear of the stuff it was easy.

She seemed to slide out then. We laid her on the ground; covered with liquid cement, she looked like she'd been dipped in mud.

But even so, there wasn't time to waste. There were four more pallbearers, I remembered, and we didn't know where they were. Maybe they were on the way back to the house right now.

'We got no time to waste, Dan,' I said. 'We gotta get outta here.'

'Who's that,' he said, pointing, and his throat was husky. Yeah, June was there, flopped in the coal, covered with filth and her grotesquely cropped head looking frighteningly obscene.

I just gave her a quick glance. I didn't like looking at her.

'That's June,' I said. 'And we gotta get outta here quickly. Go grab the car and drive it up around front. I'll get the girls upstairs meanwhile. And watch out for those pallbearers There's four of them, and they may be around somewhere.'

Dan went off and I went back to Sally. 'How are ya, kid?' I asked.

She managed to smile for me. It was a weak smile, but it did things to me. I picked her up in my arms and, covered in cement like she was, I gathered her to me. It was a funny kinda embrace. She was cold and damp, and when her arms went around my neck it felt like gigantic snails were crawling over me. But I loved it.

But we hadn't time for that. I picked her up in my arms and carried her upstairs. I sat her down in the hall, whipped a couple of overcoats off the stand and draped them round her. Then I went downstairs for June.

She was still drugged. Just like before, she was breathing so gently I could hardly tell she was still alive. I picked her up in my arms and tried not to look at that monstrous, almost bald head as it hung limply over my arms. As long as I didn't look at her hairless head it was all right. The rest of her was all right I mean. Apart from the coal dust and the grime and the ugly red blotches under her breast where the hypodermic had been thrust home time and again.

I got her upstairs and propped her on a chair beside Sally. Sally looked at her and shuddered. 'Dan'll be here in a minute,' I told her.

I went downstairs again and looked around. Uncle Taylor was done for. He'd got two slugs in his guts and another through his heart. Dr Spiller wasn't pleasant to see. I wanted to be sick when I saw all the grey white matter oozing through the jagged hole in the back of his head. One of the pallbearers would never carry a gun or a casket again, and the one I'd shot was unconscious, losing a lotta blood through the hole in his shoulder. It was a nasty wound. I did what I could for him; plugged the wound to stop the bleeding and bandaged it with a piece of his shirt. That was all there was to do.

I went upstairs again just as Dan arrived.

'I've got the car,' he said.

I motioned towards June. 'That's your pigeon,' I said.

Ugly-puss looked at her. A shudder ran through him. He looked at me. 'Jeezus,' he said, 'ain't she ugly!'

I laughed. He didn't know why I laughed. But it was funny to me hearing him call somebody ugly. 'Never mind,' I said. 'Let's get going while we can.'

He carried June to the car and thrust her in the back seat, while I pushed Sally into the back and covered her with coats so she'd warm up. Dan went around to the driving seat. I got in beside Sally.

'Where to?' asked Dan.

I thought for a minute. 'Look,' I said. 'You know this neck of the woods. Is there some kinda log cabin tucked away from everywhere, where we could lie low for a coupla days?'

'Sure,' he said. 'But what about telling the cops.'

'We ain't gonna tell the cops,' I told him.

He looked over his shoulder at me, bug-eyed. The nose of the car began to slide over to the far kerb.

'Watch it,' I yelled.

He turned around and jerked on the steering wheel.

I said: 'There's nothing to tell the cops now. Most of them fellas back there ain't gonna get near the chair on account of they've handed in their checks. Most the cops can do now is ask a lotta questions and give us a grilling.'

'I don't like cops,' said Dan.

'Me neither.'

'What about June?' he asked.

'She's worth ten grand to you,' I told him.

'Yeah, how come?'

'That's what her pa will put up for any guy giving information leading to her rescue.'

'We got the dame,' he said. 'So we go claim the reward?'

I gave a grim chuckle. 'Millionaires are notoriously mean. I guess it's because they've got a mean streak that they've got millions. Ordinary guys without a mean streak never get around to have millions.'

'So?'

'So, fella, when you turn up at Miller's place with June, since he employed you to look after him, he may kinda take the view that you ain't entitled to receive the reward. He'll welsh on you.'

'He would, too, the mean skunk, if he got half a chance.'

'We won't give him that chance. Just you drive off to that log cabin and I'll do the rest. And stop when we pass a camera shop.'

It was hot in the car. It was so hot that Sally's slimy covering was steaming and powdering off her. I helped her brush it off, and the more the cement was cleaned off, the more of Sally came to light.

She hadn't been wearing many clothes to start with, on account of the hot weather. And when we'd had that tug of war with the cement, her clothes hadn't been equal to the strain. Some parts of her clothes still stuck to her. The rest of them had remained in the hole with the cement.

I got enthusiastic about brushing off that cement.

'Hank,' she said, with a sparkle in her eye.

I stopped brushing cement from a certain part of her anatomy and looked sheepish.

'It's nice of you to help, Hank,' she smiled. 'But it's not quite the time …!' She looked meaningfully at Dan, whose ears turned red. He'd been glancing at the reflection in the driving mirror.

I grinned, wrapped one of the overcoats around her and pulled her close to me.

She said: 'What about June?'

Hell, I'd forgotten about her. I turned around to her. She was slumped in the seat with her limbs hanging gee-gaw. Her mouth was hanging open and the little sprouts of hair on her cropped head still looked obscene.

I looked at another part of her. It was worth looking at. This June girl had everything once she had her hair. Sally slipped her hands around my head and closed my eyes. 'Naughty, naughty,' she whispered.

'I wasn't exactly looking,' I protested. 'I was just looking her over to see how she is. Like a doctor would look her over.'

'If a doctor ever starts looking me over in that way, I'll start screaming for help.'

'Jealous?'

'No. Not jealous. Just wondering what a million dollar dame has got that I haven't.'

'Nothing,' I said emphatically.

'Except a million dollars,' she added *sotto voce*.

'I'll take you without the million bucks.'

'You'll have to.'

That reminded me about Uncle Taylor. 'What happened? Did your uncle and Spiller finally quarrel?'

'I think Uncle must have finally got his courage together when be realised I was going to be buried. Another five minutes and they'd have covered me in. But Uncle got that gun from somewhere.'

'He certainly saved the situation.'

She was very solemn for a few moments. 'Uncle was being blackmailed by Spiller,' she said.

'Yeah, I guessed that. I got a private eye to check up that angle for me. Things happened so fast, I ain't had time to check with him.'

'S'you think June's all right?' she asked.

I gave another look at June, suppressed the inevitable shudder, and put my hand over her heart. It was beating softly. Her skin was soft, too, I noticed.

'Ahem,' said Sally, meaningfully.

I made an effort, lifted my eyes and pulled back the lid of June's eyes, exposing the pupil. The pupil was a pin-point.

I slapped her face. It was like slapping the wall for all the impression it made.

'How often did Doctor Spiller give her an injection?'

'About every twelve hours.'

'How long since the last injection ?'

'Couple of hours.'

'Jeezus,' I said. 'She'll probably be cold like this until tonight.'

'If you wanna get yourself a camera,' yelled Dan, 'this is the place. Though what the hell you want a camera for, I can't think.'

'You get out and buy it,' I said. 'Get a good one with time exposure.' I rolled a coupla century notes off my wad and gave them to him. Then I slung an overcoat over June. If anyone was liable to get curious and poke his nose in the car, I didn't want him to see what looked like a scalped stiff.

Dan got the camera. It was just the type I wanted. And a few minutes later, we were heading out into the open country.

12

Dan certainly justified once being described as 'The Boy from Iowa.' He certainly knew the State.

He nosed out a hunting cabin parked miles from anywhere in hilly woodland.

It was a beautiful spot. A shallow river chuckled over the stones by the side of the cabin, and we could get a good view across the countryside. That was useful. The countryside was beautiful to look at. But at the same time, we could see a long way off when anybody looked like dropping in and joining us for tea.

It was getting dusk when we arrived. The cabin was barely furnished, and lighted by oil-lamps. After we'd piled outta the car, brought in the provisions that we'd collected *en route* and Sally had got busy tidying the place up, it began to be quite homely. Sally looked cute with a coloured blanket pinned around her on the style of a sarong. She had to wear something like that, because her own clothes were literally nothing to speak of, and poor Dan was getting a crick in his neck trying to be a gentleman and not look at her.

Sally got busy with the frying pan and some cans of beans, and after we'd eaten a good meal, enjoyed a cigarette and walloped a few quarts of beer, we began to feel very much better.

The cabin was snug and compact. The living-room-cum-kitchen was large and two smaller rooms led off. These were the bedrooms and they contained wooden bunks fitted against the wall.

We'd shoved June on one of the bunks. Midway through my second after-dinner cigarette, we heard a kinda moan from June's room. I looked at Dan and got up. He and Sally followed me. June's face lad lost its calmness; unsuspected muscles were causing her lips and eyes to twitch. There was warmth in her face now and she was breathing more loudly.

'Get some brandy,' I said.

Dan came back with some brandy and we fed it to June. We worked hard on her for about half an hour before she came round. I was feeling sorry for that dame. She'd been drugged into unconsciousness for something like three days, and the only time she'd been conscious was when Spiller had brought her round in order to give her the hot foot.

She was lying with her grotesque head pillowed in Sally's lap. Dan was rubbing her hands to keep the circulation moving, and I was forcing brandy between her lips. She gave a little moan. 'Wake up, June,' I said.

She moaned again.

'Wake up,' I urged. 'You've been asleep a long while.' Her eyelids fluttered with the effort she was making to climb up into consciousness.

'Talk to me, June,' I said.

And then, not long after that, she finally did come around.

Her eyes looked up into mine, and they were filled with pain and horror.

'Where am I?'

'You're okay,' I said. 'You're with friends.'

She looked like she was trying to remember.

'You're with friends,' I insisted. 'We took you away from that cellar.'

Her eyes widened then, as the memory of that last phase of her consciousness came home to her. Her eyes went crazy and she started to scream, madly.

I slapped her face hard. I kept on slapping until the pain of it stabbed through the fear. She lay back exhausted, looking up at me.

'You're all right, now, June,' I told her. 'You can go home to your father now.'

She said suddenly: 'My ear … they didn't …'

She tried to raise her hand, but Dan was holding it tightly. I said quickly: 'You're all right, June. They haven't harmed you.'

She didn't believe me. I could see it in her eyes. She tore her hand away from Dan and felt for her ear. Relief flooded into her face as she made sure both ears were intact. Then surprise followed as she missed something. Her hand went to her head, feeling for her hair. And then, when she realised what had happened, there was some more screaming.

That bout of screaming and crying went on and on. Dan and I cleared out into the living room and left Sally trying to comfort her. June kept moaning over and over again: 'My hair … my hair … where is it?'

I sat on the back two legs of the kitchen chair and poured another glass of beer for myself.

'I'm gonna take a trip tomorrow,' I told Dan.

'You ain't gonna leave me here with those two dames?'

'Sure I am. You'll be okay. But the way I've got

things figured, you're gonna be here for a while yet.'

'Yeah, how long?'

'Maybe a month. Maybe two months.'

'I don't figure on that,' he said.

'You will, Dan. Just you wait till June gets calm enough to talk sensibly and you'll see. I've got this thing figured out from A to Z. That's one of the reasons why I took those photographs of June.'

He scratched his head. 'What's going on in your mind?'

'Don't get impatient, fella. You'll see in good time.'.

It was round about midnight before June was in any state to sit up and talk sensibly. Lots of things had happened meanwhile. First of all, she'd looked at herself in the mirror. That'd started the screaming all over again. I wasn't surprised. It must have been a shock to see herself looking that way. Then she'd had to get some grub inside her, and since she hadn't eaten a thing in something like three days, there was a pretty good chance that she was gonna be sick or something.

And finally she had to wash. She was covered in dirt and coal dust, and it had eaten into the pores of her skin. Sally went to work like a Trojan with pails of water and pans and soap and heaven knows what. And finally June emerged from the bedroom with a blanket pinned up around her like Sally's and a towel turban that, swathed around her head, restored her to what she used to look like before Dr Spiller got to work on her.

I offered her some beer. She refused curtly. She was holding herself in with an effort. A doll with three blind eyes could see she was all strung up and liable to snap her sanity cord at any moment. I wasn't surprised. Not after all she'd been through.

I said: 'Look, June, we're gonna tell you exactly what's happened, up to the present moment. After that, you'll have to make some decisions.'

She said, 'God,' quietly, and rested her head in her hand.

'You gotta listen, June,' I said.

'I know. I'm just all strung up, I guess.'

I told her everything that had happened, how she'd been hidden in the casket and taken to Thornvale, and how her hair had been cut off to send to her father. When I got to that part, I thought she'd start crying again. But she didn't. She'd taken a grip on herself. Then I went on and told her how Dan and I had got her loose and how there'd been a gunfight and how those fellas had got theirs.

When I'd finished, she said: 'Why did you bring me here? Why didn't you take me home? Father will be worried about me.'

I said: 'I got reasons. Good reasons. The first is this: how would you like me to take you back home? You know what it'd be like, thousands of news-hawks, cameras flashing, big headlines in the newspapers.' I paused, meaningfully. Then I said: 'How would you like to become America's number one hairless woman? How would you like photographs spread all over the news-sheets? You've looked in the mirror. You know what you look like?'

She shuddered. Partly in horror, partly with self-pity.

'I wanted to save you from that,' I told her.

She looked up quickly. 'Can you do something?'

'It's easy. Tomorrow I'm gonna see your father. I'm gonna tell him exactly what's happened. You can send him a note, and there's a photograph I've taken of you so he can see how you look now. Then it's all up to him.'

'You'll do that?' she pleaded.

'Sure I'll do it. Your father can tell some yarn that you fell off the train unhurt, lost your memory and turned up down in Florida, and you're gonna stop there for a few months. Meantime you can stop on here until your hair grows out again.'

'Will it take long?' she asked anxiously.

'Might do,' said Sally. 'Thing for you to do is to keep your head uncovered, get the fresh air and sun to your head. If you go around all the time with your hair wrapped up that way, the chances are it'll never grow again.'

June began to cry again. I looked at Dan. He got up and I got up. We went outside and took a walk. This crying business was getting a bit too much for us.

Early next morning, I set off in the hire car for Des Moines. It was a good run and I didn't arrive until early afternoon. I found out where Miller lived and went to his millionaire's paradise. There were cops posted all over the place and lots of secretaries and butlers all wanting to know my business and what I'd come about.

I stuck to my simple story that I was a friend of Dan Rutland's, that I'd met Mr Miller and I wanted to see him about something very personal and very private.

It was about an hour before they gave up trying to break me down and get me to spout my business, and finally I got shown into Miller's spacious office.

He recognised me straight off. 'You were on that train,' he said. 'The train June was on when she disappeared.'

I'll say this for the fella. He did seem mighty cut up

about losing his daughter. The bags under his eyes showed that he hadn't slept for days, and his nerves were cut ragged.

I said: 'I want to talk to you personal.'

'It's about June?' he asked, and leaned across the table anxiously.

'It's about something else,' I said.

'Oh.' He slumped in his seat and seemed to lose interest in my presence.

'Can I talk to you in private ?' I asked.

'Hmm? Oh. Yes, go ahead.'

'Nobody listening?' I pressed him.

'No, nobody's here.' Something about my attitude was gaining his interest again.

I got up and walked around to his side of the desk. There was a thin wire running down by his knee. I got my fingers under the wire and jerked hard. Then I traced the broken end while Miller looked at me with his cheeks swollen in apoplexy. As I had suspected, there was a small microphone hidden under the desk. It was either for the benefit of a confidential secretary or for a Dictaphone.

Miller spluttered indignantly. 'Of all the infernal …'

I said grimly: 'Look, Miller, when a fella wants to talk to you on a life and death matter, and when it's in confidence, don't try to be clever. It don't pay.'

'I'll have you thrown out,' he said.

'I know where June is,' I told him.

'What?' He grabbed hold of the edge of the desk, and he was trembling with excitement.

'I know where June is,' I told him again. 'And I've come to talk to you about things.'

'You want money?' he said. 'I'll pay anything,

anything, if only you'll get her back.'

I reached out to his cigar box, selected a fat Havana, sat in his deep chair and struck a match. Miller jittered pm the other side of the desk. 'Tell me,' he said. 'What is it?'

'Sit down,' I said. 'This is gonna be a long story and it's gonna take a long time. Don't you worry about June, though. She's okay.'

He could see I meant what I said, so he sat on the edge of his chair and watched me with large, expectant eyes like he was a little dog waiting for a tit-bit.

I said: 'You gotta listen without interruption. Ask questions later if you want. But hear what I got to say, first. Understand?'

'Yes,' he said quickly, 'I understand.'

'Good.' I took a long pull at that very excellent cigar and, starting from the beginning, I told him everything that had happened. He was as good as his word. When I'd finished, he looked at me, his face white.

'You've come from them,' he said. 'You've killed her.'

I moved uneasily. 'Look, fella. This is from June. It's her writing and you can see the date. It's yesterday's date.'

He read through the note. But he didn't look any easier.

'I gotta note signed by her,' he said. 'It was her handwriting. You say she got the hot foot signing that. Maybe she got a lot more hot foots before she wrote this one.'

This guy was getting me mad. He was as suspicious as a wagon-load of monkeys. And what the hell was I to get from this anyway?

'Look, Miller,' I said. 'What am I getting outta this

? If I'm telling you a tale, what's my angle? How do I cash in?'

That argument appealed to him. He saw the logic of it. He thought about it. He gave it great consideration, and either way he looked at it I didn't stand to make a bean. That convinced him. He began to believe that maybe I was telling the truth.

'What do you want me to do?' he asked.

I said: 'It ain't what I wancher to do. It's what your daughter wants. Right now she's sitting snugly in a little cabin with Dan Rutland acting watchdog over her. She's safe and she's not hurt. The only thing wrong with her is a slight case of baldness. I'm telling you, June don't wanna come outta that hideout until her hair's grown good and long again.'

'That's crazy,' he said.

I pulled out the photos I'd taken of her. He gazed at then incredulously and then with horror.

'You see what I mean?' I said. 'Mo dame wants her face in the papers when she's looking that way.'

He swallowed. 'It doesn't look like her right away, does it?'

'It doesn't make her look like a glamour girl exactly.'

'All right,' he agreed. 'What do you want me to do about the cops? They're looking all over for her.'

'You're a man of influence. Spread a few bucks around among the cops. Get them to switch off the heat. Tell them you've had word from June. She's turned up in Florida and is stopping right there on holiday. Tell any damn story you like. Say she fell off the train, caught a dose of amnesia from a blow on the head and walked away and picked up a lift to Florida. Say any damn thing you please that'll keep the cops and the news-hawks quiet.'

'I can do that,' he said. 'But I wanna see June. How is she?'

'You can see her. Get the cops quiet first and then you can see her. If you try seeing her now, every cub reporter for forty miles around will be following you to see where you're heading.'

'Yes,' he agreed. 'I see your point.'

'There's one thing more,' I said.

'Well?'

'Dan Rutland. He saved June. He got her away from the snatchers.'

'So he ought. He was employed to guard her. He should never have lost her in the first place.'

'That ain't quite the way it was. He was employed to keep his eyes on you. He was your bodyguard. Naturally he'd have looked after June as well. But he couldn't be in two places at once, could he ?'

'What are you driving at?'

'You were offering a reward of ten grand to any guy that gave help to find your daughter. Dan did better. He actually saved her. He's entitled to that ten grand.'

'I won't pay him,' said Miller.

'I figured you'd wriggle, you chiselling little hound,' I said. 'As soon as you learn your daughter's safe, you want to start in on saving a few measly dollars.'

'I'll talk to Rutland about it,' he glared.

'No you won't, you'll talk to me.'

'I'll not discuss the matter any further.'

'In that case, I won't. I'll just take action.' I pulled the photographs from my pocket again. 'I reckon the *Daily Sun* will pay ten grand for these photos. I'll pass the dough over to Dan.'

Miller almost choked. 'I get it now,' he said.

'You're trying to get money out of me with a yarn. None of this is true. You just want ten thousand easy money.'

'Keep your hair on,' I said 'You don't have to part with any dough … yet. You just sign a note saying that when your daughter June returns home with Dan Rutland, you'll promise to pay Dan Rutland the sum of ten grand. That should make you feel better. If your daughter doesn't come home safe with Dan Rutland, then that paper'll be no use to anybody.'

He glared at me, muttered under his breath and pulled a sheet of paper from his desk drawer. He wrote very rapidly in a scrawly handwriting with a pen that musta cost enough to take me to the continent for a year's holiday. When he'd finished writing, he read it through, signed it and skimmed the paper across the desk at me.

I picked it up. It read okay. I folded it and shoved it in my pocket.

I said: 'Get the heat taken off, get the newspapers to pipe down, and then meet me in Mason City outside the Courtalds Bank in three days from now. Make it noon when you get there. And make sure nobody knows where you're going, else your daughter's gonna find herself a lotta unpleasant publicity.'

After I'd left the joint, I called around at the hotel where I'd left my own car. I couldn't really do without that car of mine. Fitted up the way it was, and full of all the equipment I needed for a long camping trip, I certainly wanted it now.

I made arrangements with the hotel people to return the hire car to Mason City. They said they'd paid some bum to drive it all the way there for me.

Then I filled up with gas and started off again on the long run back to the cabin. But before I left Des Moines, I did a deal of shopping. There were many extras that were wanted if that cabin was gonna be lived in for a time.

So it was nightfall when I got back to the cabin. But I was loaded down with goods and there was great excitement among the two girls when they saw the clothes I'd bought. They were getting tired of dragging around in blanket robes. It musta been hot, too, up there in the woods with the sun beating down.

So the next coupla days we lazed around, sun-bathing, playing cards, lying in the stream in bathing costumes. June had got used to me and Dan being around and she didn't mind so much us seeing what her head looked like. But there was something about that cropped head that made me feel sick. I tried to hide my feelings and Dan tried to hide his too. But he musta felt the same way about it as I did. Just as long as June was prancing around with her cropped head sticking out like a sore thumb, we just had to make an effort not to look away from her with disgust written across our faces.

On the day appointed, I went down early to Mason City to meet June's father. I brought him up to the cabin and he stopped for about an hour. He was pleased to see June. But he didn't much like seeing her the way she was. I guess it kinda made him sick the way it made us sick.

She'd got used to having just the three of us around; Sally, Dan and me, that is. Her father was the first person apart from us who'd seen her this way. When she saw how her father reacted, it started her off all over again. She ran into the bedroom and sobbed her heart out. He didn't stop long after that. He just wanted to be off to attend to his business. It was I who had to remind him about financial matters.

'You know, Dan's gotta be paid for looking after June. I ain't saying that any guy is liable to want her, seeing that she's looking the way she is. But you never can tell. Some guy might get some idea as to who she really is, and that's where Dan is gonna be useful.'

'I'll continue to pay him,' said Miller.

'Thanks, boss,' said Dan, as though Miller was doing him a favour.

'And he gets the ten grand ?'

'Sure he does,' said Miller, but he looked pretty mean about it.

'What say we write Dan a cheque now, huh?'

Miller glared. I tapped my pocket meaningfully, the pocket where I kept the photos. Miller gave a snort, pulled out his cheque book.

I said: 'Make it all out at one go, the ten grand, two months' salary and the rent on this cabin. I'm gonna rent it for three months, just in case somebody else gets the feeling they'd like a little loneliness and tries booking up the place.

Dan got his cheque, Miller said farewell to his daughter and I took him back to Mason City. 'Dan'll get in touch with you when June wants to come back,' I told him.

13

When I got back to the cabin, I took Sally on one side, 'Look,' I said. 'I've been going into things while I was in town.'

'About my uncle?'

'Yeah. Seems the cops got busy investigating when the tradesmen reported finding the door open. They found the bodies and are looking for a lead to find out what happened. But they seem all set to figure it as a shooting match.'

'It's going to be difficult for me to go back,' she said.

'You ain't going back,' I told her

'What d'ya mean, Hank?'

I said: 'There's nothing to go back to. While I was in town, I spent some time with that private eye I told you about. He got me a loada dirt on your uncle and Dr Spiller. Seems like your uncle's been plunging on the Stock Exchange with the dough that was in his trust for you. Dr Spiller was right there behind him, using the money and trying to make a fortune. When financial arrangements didn't work out the way they wanted, it gave Dr Spiller the thumb on your uncle. You can use your imagination as to how Spiller induced your uncle to take part in the snatch plan and the plan to get rid of you, so as it wouldn't have to be exposed that you've lost your inheritance.'

'There's no money for me, then?' she said simply.

'Not a dime. Even the house is mortgaged up to the hilt.'

'I'll be able to get along,' she said.

'Sure you will. You've got me with you.'

She held my arm. 'You do want me with you, don't you, Hank?'

I put my arms around her and squeezed tightly. 'Sure I wancher. I guess I've been waiting all my life to meet you. I ain't gonna lose hold of you now.'

She said: 'How long do we stop here?'

'We'll stay until June's hair grows out again.'

'It's a bit crowded with Dan and June, isn't it?'

I looked at her, wonderingly. Her eyes danced. She said: 'With you and Dan in one bedroom and me and June in the other, it makes things a bit awkward, doesn't it?'

'It kinda does make things awkward,' I replied. 'Dan can't be in the room with June because she's in the room with you, and you can't be in the room with me because Dan's in the room with me. A kinda vicious circle.'

'A change from the eternal triangle,' she wisecracked.

'Because Dan and me are square guys.'

'Sharp fella.'

'Yeah,' I said. 'I've been eating razor-blades.'

'You look pretty cut-up.'

'But at any rate, I've found a way to get rid of the old blades.'

'Let's get outta here,' she said. 'Let's go some place where we can be alone together.'

'That suits me.'

We walked back to the log cabin, and when we get inside Dan was at the sink, washing up. June was sitting back in a chair reading a book. Dan's hands weren't made for washing up. They were made for punching a path to stardom. Just as we got inside, one of the cups slid from his hand and smashed on the floor.

'You clumsy big oaf,' June mouthed at him. 'Isn't there anything you can do the right way?'

'I'm sorry, Miss June,' he said, flushing and ashamed of himself.

That's the way it had been between them all the time. June might have been a good-looker when she had her hair on. But she had the conscience and the manners of a pig. Dan was a paid employee and she regarded him as a slave, and therefore contemptible. She was just about the most piggish dame I'd ever met. She didn't try anything on with me, because she knew I'd get tough about it. But Dan was a good-natured fella. Dan was a real sucker for her venom and her despicable behaviour. And Dan went on taking it. He'd been taking it like that ever since we'd been in the cabin. It made me sick to see it happening. But there wasn't much that could be done about it.

I said: 'All right, can the big 'I am' stuff, Jane. If you can't treat Dan like he's a human being, at any rate stop getting at him all the time.'

She tried to toss her head at me. But it didn't come off. She'd have made a pretty good show if she'd had her hair. But she hadn't, and the result of her action was to make her look pretty silly.

I grinned. Sally tried to suppress a smile, and Dan

said: 'Creepers, don't she look queer that way.'

June flew into a rage. She slung a jug off the table at Dan. He dodged and it smashed against the wall beside his head. She'd have probably thrown a lot of other things and Dan would probably have gone on dodging them if I hadn't stepped in and grabbed her.

I said: 'Look, you two. You'd better start getting sociable, because you ain't gonna have no other company around.'

'You ain't leaving, are you, Hank?' said Dan. He sounded scared.

'Me and Sally are clearing out,' I told him. 'We're gonna take a little trip together.'

'Gee,' he said. He looked at June, looked at her cropped head and shuddered. 'You gonna leave me alone with her?' he said. 'She gives me the creeps.'

Luckily I was standing right behind June, and I was able to grab her when she started throwing things again. And then, after she'd quietened down, I said to Sally: 'Okay, honey, get your things packed.'

Dan looked at me with a sorrowful expression on his ugly face. 'Gee, Hank,' he said pathetically.

I said: 'Look fella, come outside. I wanna talk with you.'

We went outside and walked down into the woods. I said: 'D'you want some good advice?'

'You've helped me a lot. Anything you say is okay by me.

'You're letting that June make a monkey outta you.'

'I know,' he said. 'But that's the way things are. She's that kinda dame. What can you do with a dame like that?'

'Give her a damn good spanking.'

'That's what she needs,' he agreed. 'But honest, Hank, I can't get tough with a dame. If it's a fella now ...'

'That's your trouble,' I said. 'You've been brought up in the old school. You think women have gotta be treated gentle and polite all the time. But wake up, Dan. That line's okay with dames that have got something to their credit. But this dame's a pain in the neck. All her life she's had what she's wanted. She's got no more regard for human feelings than she has for a train-line. What you gotta do, Dan, is to show her that human beings are human beings.'

'I'd like to get tough with her, Hank. Sometimes she makes me so mad I wanna take her apart. But you can't treat a dame that way.'

'Nonsense,' I said. 'There's some dames that need slapping around. And the fella that does it is doing them a favour. It might make all the difference to their life.'

His big eyes looked at me seriously. 'You really mean it, Hank? You really think I should teach that dame a lesson?'

'What have I been telling you for the past ten minutes?'

He thought about it. The idea was new to him. And when he churned it over in his mind, he could see the possibilities.

I said: 'It's a piece of cake for you. She's stuck here with you for at least a coupla months. That's a long while to be shut away with somebody. Are you gonna do those two months the smart way or the tough way?'

'I think you got something, fella,' he said.

'Attaboy.' I felt in my pocket and brought out the photographs. 'Just as a little extra encouragement to her to be good, you can wave these around in front of her. Tell her that you know a fella that'd like to give these to his editor.'

'I'll take those,' he said. 'Maybe they'll come in useful later. Right now I'll try without using them.'

We walked back to the cabin. 'You wanna make a start now,' I said.

'Yeah. I'd like that. I'll feel better if I know you're around.'

'I'll be right behind you. And remember, every time you feel like backing down, I'm right there watching you. I don't think you're yella, Dan. Just prove it to me, willya?'

'Course, if she gets tough, it won't be like fighting a fella,' he said.

'No,' I said. 'You gotta develop a new technique. You just leave it to instinct. You'll find out what to do, right enough.'

We went back to the cabin. Sally was already packed and waiting for me to come back.

June was sitting back in the chair with a magazine across her lap. She said airily to me: 'Well, I'm much obliged for the help you gave me. I guess my father paid you plenty for it. That'll help you on your way.'

I stood in front of her and said levelly: 'Listen, Miss June, I ain't received a penny from your father, and if he offered it to me, which I doubt, I wouldn't accept anything. Maybe I did help you outta a jam. So did Dan here. But has it ever occurred to you that we did that just so we could be useful to somebody?'

'Yeah, but you coulda got some dough outta Dad.'

I said slowly: 'Your dad can go to hell, his money can go to hell and you can go to hell as well. And while I'm about it, let me tell you what I think of you. I think you're the miserablest, most worthless slut I've ever met.'

She sat bolt upright in her chair, her eyes flaming, and the cropped scrub of her hair seamed to bristle. 'You insulting swine,' she mouthed. 'How dare you speak to me like that.'

Dan hitched his trousers uneasily. I'd given him a lead and this was his chance. He said: 'Don't you go talking to Hank that way. I guess everything he said is right.'

June may have been scared of me, but Dan was a different proposition – she thought. She got up outta her chair with a slow, menacing movement. Her eyes were slits and her fingers crooked like talons. Hairless the way she was, this made her look just about the most repulsive thing I've ever seen.

She advanced slowly towards Dan, her lips writhing and curling back over her sharp teeth. Mad viciousness expressed itself in every taut line of her body.

'You scum,' she mouthed at Dan. 'How dare you talk to me that way?'

Normally maybe, Dan would have backed away. But now he stood his ground. He looked uneasy, but he did stand his ground. June went right up close to him, and then one of her hands shot out like a raking claw. Blood spurted from his cheek as nails shredded skin from his face.

June musta been surprised at Dan then. He caught her hand, spun her around and shoved her so that she went flying across the room to bang against the wall. But if she was surprised, she was much more angry. It was a maddening insult to her that Dan should have treated her in the way she asked to be treated. She turned and rushed at him. Sally made a movement as though she was trying to stop her. I grabbed Sally by the arm. 'Leave them to it,' I said. 'Let Dan settle this his way.'

I watched them as June, mad with rage, flung herself at Dan. He caught her by the hands, swung her around and shoved her towards the wall for the second time.

June was good for a long while yet. She turned, ran at Dan, and at the last moment kicked him in the groin. It was a vicious kick, and June didn't know it but Dan had got himself a bad rupture through a blow like that. Dan doubled up in agony. June picked up a table and smashed it on his head. Dan crumpled up on the floor. He wasn't unconscious, but he was badly dazed.

I resisted an impulse to do something to try to help Dan. This was his trouble and he'd have to deal with it himself.

June started in kicking him. She couldn't hurt him much, because she was wearing high-heeled sandals and they wouldn't hurt a tough guy like Dan, provided it was his side or his shoulders she was kicking. Dan was still groaning, but I could see he was recovering. And then he reached out, grabbed June's ankle and jerked. She came down hard on her fanny with a bump that shook the floorboards. And when she came down, she squealed like a stuck pig. Dan reached out and wrapped his hands around her mouth. She clawed at his hands, and long bloody streaks of gouted blood across the backs of his hands.

I guess that was when Dan entered into the spirit of the thing He let go of her and slapped her face. She slapped back. But whereas her palm bounced off Dan's face, her cheeks were stained red, smarted so the tears ran down her face.

'You beast,' she raged.

Dan got up slowly. She got up slowly. Then her

eyes ran around the room wildly. There was a cane chair nearby. She snatched that up and brought it down with all her strength on Dan's upraised arm. He got hold of her by the shoulder and she jerked away. She left most of the top part of her dress in his hands. Her soft breasts curved invitingly.

Up went the chair again, and this time it splintered against Dan's arm. He was tough, that guy. And when he grabbed at June, he didn't miss. He grabbed her good and hard. She struggled like a wildcat, but in his strong arms she was like a child. He twisted her over his knee and then he spanked her. He spanked her with the ease and assurance that a parent smacks a naughty child, but there was a lot more steam behind his slaps. He was slapping to hurt and he meant to hurt.

June was wearing only a thin frock, and that didn't muffle the slaps any. At first, June kicked her legs and screamed with the humiliation and indignity of being slapped. After that she began to scream, because she was being hurt, and then finally she slumped into a kinda stunned acceptance, sobbing and moaning, her body jerking painfully every time Dan brought his hand down. But it took quite a while to get to that stage.

I've seen some spankings in my time, but I don't think I've ever seen anybody so soundly spanked before. Dan went on slapping, it seemed never-endingly. And every time his large hand came down, it had plenty of steam behind it. But by the time he was finally through, he was good and tired. His shirt was soaked beneath the armpits. And when he was through, he just let June roll on the floor, where she lay and sobbed.

'I think,' said Dan, 'that we'll have a drink all round.'

'I'm all with you. You've given that dame what

she's been needing for longer than I can reckon.'

'She ain't going to like that,' said Sally. But I could see by her eyes that she thought June deserved it.

'She's gonna like that,' said Dan determinedly. 'If she don't, she'll get the same again until she does.' He was completely sure of himself now. 'Get up,' he said to June.

June lay there and whimpered. Dan bent down, grabbed her by what was left of the dress and pulled her to her feet.

'Get some drinks,' he said.

June whimpered.

Dan bent her around, twisted her, got her across his knee again. 'Gonna get those drinks?' he said.

June gulped. 'I'll get them, you bully,' she said.

She did, too. We sat there while June got the whisky bottle and set up the glasses. We smoked a coupla cigarettes and drank and talked, and all the time June sat there quietly, broodingly, looking at Dan with a strange expression in her eyes.

And she was still watching him like that when Sally and I got into my car and drove off.

Sally and I had a kinda extended honeymoon that lasted a coupla months. The only thing we didn't have was a wedding. But Sally was broadminded and I am too, and we kinda felt we oughtta know each other real well before we threw halters around each other's necks.

But we got along well during those two months, travelling around and enjoying things together. And as we had promised, at the end of two months we went back to the cabin.

There was a pleasant homeliness about it when we

got there. The chimney was smoking, linen was hanging on a line to dry and Dan was chopping firewood.

When we went inside, June was standing over by the sink, soap lather all the way up her arms. There was a radiant look in her eyes, and somehow she seemed soft and different. Her hair had grown, too. It was by now a very short bob, and it was quite enough to begin to make June look really interesting.

'Busy?' asked Sally.

June wiped her forearm across her forehead. 'Washing Dan's socks,' she explained. 'He's dreadfully heavy on socks.'

'Fancy that,' I drawled. My voice probably suggested I'd never dreamed she could do anything that was useful.

'She's a fine cook, too,' said Dan defensively.

'I'm not arguing about it,' I said. 'You oughtta know. You've been having it for the last two months.'

'I'm gonna go on having it, too,' said Dan.

I looked at him in amazement. June came up behind him, and he slipped his arm around her waist. She looked up into his ugly face, and her eyes were shining and sparkling. She had the face of a very happy woman.

'So that's the way it is?' I said.

'I like it good,' said Dan.

'I like it, too,' said June.

'I know one guy who ain't gonna like it,' I said.

'You mean father?'

'Yeah, just wait till father hears.'

June smiled up into Dan's face again. 'We don't care. We're gonna live here anyway. We like it here.'

I looked at Sally. She looked at me. I said: 'Say, honey, d'ya kind of get the feeling we're superfluous around here?'

'Let's leave them,' she said.

We climbed back into the car; I let in the clutch.

'Will you be best man?' Dan yelled.

'Sure. Send me a letter care of the Post Office. If it reaches me, I'll come and be your best man.'

'Bye,' called Sally.

'Bye,' called June.

I drove out through the trees, got on the rough road track, heading toward the main arterial road. Sally snuggled up beside me. 'I love you, darling,' she whispered.

'That's corny,' I said. 'Say something original.'

'Keplang, that's original.'

'I mean something nice.'

'Strawberries and cream,' she said.

I bent over and whispered in her ear. She closed her eyes happily and snuggled up to me closer.

'Darling,' she said in a whisper.

ALSO AVAILABLE FROM TELOS PUBLISHING

CRIME

THE LONG, BIG KISS GOODBYE
by SCOTT MONTGOMERY
Hardboiled thrills as Jack Sharp gets involved with a
dame called Kitty.

MIKE RIPLEY

Titles in Mike Ripley's acclaimed 'Angel' series of comic
crime novels.

JUST ANOTHER ANGEL by MIKE RIPLEY
ANGEL TOUCH by MIKE RIPLEY
ANGEL HUNT by MIKE RIPLEY
ANGEL ON THE INSIDE by MIKE RIPLEY
ANGEL CONFIDENTIAL by MIKE RIPLEY
ANGEL CITY by MIKE RIPLEY
ANGELS IN ARMS by MIKE RIPLEY
FAMILY OF ANGELS by MIKE RIPLEY
BOOTLEGGED ANGEL by MIKE RIPLEY
THAT ANGEL LOOK by MIKE RIPLEY

HANK JANSON

Classic pulp crime thrillers from the 1940s and 1950s.

TORMENT by HANK JANSON
WOMEN HATE TILL DEATH by HANK JANSON

SOME LOOK BETTER DEAD by HANK JANSON
SKIRTS BRING ME SORROW by HANK JANSON
WHEN DAMES GET TOUGH by HANK JANSON
ACCUSED by HANK JANSON
KILLER by HANK JANSON
FRAILS CAN BE SO TOUGH by HANK JANSON
BROADS DON'T SCARE EASY by HANK JANSON
KILL HER IF YOU CAN by HANK JANSON
LILIES FOR MY LOVELY by HANK JANSON
BLONDE ON THE SPOT by HANK JANSON
THIS WOMAN IS DEATH by HANK JANSON
THE LADY HAS A SCAR by HANK JANSON

Non-fiction

THE TRIALS OF HANK JANSON
by STEVE HOLLAND

TELOS PUBLISHING
Email: orders@telos.co.uk
Web: www.telos.co.uk

To order copies of any Telos books, please visit our website where there are full details of all titles and facilities for worldwide credit card online ordering, as well as occasional special offers.